Negative Fold

Ron Mueller

Books and Stories by Ron Mueller

The Taelo Series

Taelo: The Early Years
Taelo: The Golden Feather
Taelo: Journey of Discovery
Taelo: Dangerous Passage
Taelo: Condor Clan Slingers
Taelo: Circumvention
Taelo: The Journey of Sages
Taelo: Collection
Taelo: Future Leaders Journey

A Taelo Story:

White Swan and Quiet Pheasant
The Child's Name
Floating Cloud
Quiet Rabbit
Busy Bee
Little Otter & Talking Wren
Broken Spear
Burley Bear & Meadow Flower

Science Fiction

The Savitar Series:
    Journey's End
    Savitar
    Confluence
    Savitar Collection

Bram Nielson Series
    The Fold
    The Message
    Fold Wormhole
    Negative Fold
    Ripples in Time
    Bram Nielson Collection

Single Science Fiction Books

    Current Past and Future
    The Event
    The Door
    Viajante 7

Ron Mueller

<u>Fiction Series</u>

The Alex Evercrest Series
> The River Front
> The Girl on The Grill
> Missing
> Maggot
> Racist
> Votive Candles
> Windy City
> Country Road
> Pool of Blood
> Sins of the Daughter
> Body Parts
> The Skull Collector
> The Vanishing
> The Shadow Fighter
> Moonshine
> Grief's Trajectory
> The Magic Touch
> Northern Lights
> Alex Evercrest Heroin Collection
> Alex Evercrest Collection Two

A Brian Oneil Novell
> Hawaiian Phoenix
> Moon Curser
> Death Broker

The Problem Solver Series
> Solutions
> Drug Lords
> Border Crosser
> Problem Solver Collection

Imagination by Courtney Huynh and Chloe Parker

Negative Fold
By: *Ron Mueller*

Around the World Publishing LLC
4914 Cooper Road Suite 144
Cincinnati, Ohio 45242-9998

This story is a work of fiction. Names,
characters, places, and incidents either are
products of the author's imagination or are
used fictitiously. Any resemblance to actual
events or locales or persons, living or dead,
is entirely coincidental.

Negative Fold, by Ron Mueller Copyright © 2022
Renewed 2024

ISBN 13: 978-1-68223-277-4
ISBN 10: 1-68223-277-8

Distributed by Ingram
Cover Picture by: NASA @ShutterStock
Cover Design by: Ron Mueller

Ron Mueller

Dedicated to those

open to a new understanding

of the Universe.

Table of Content

Ron Mueller

Chapter 1: Growing Old, Growing Bold

Bram was going through his morning wake up preparation. He was standing in front of the mirror shaving and thinking about the "Negative Fold Universe." This was an accidental discovery made while he worked on what he now thought of as "The Positive Fold Universe" equation. He had been working on a way to move a Fold transport bubble in both the forward and reverse direction.

To go forward he had incremented time in each part of his Fold equation. He had done this by incrementing all the time components of the Fold equation in unison.

He discovered and had come to the realization that to go in reverse, he had to decrement time. This required one forward control program and a separate reverse control program.

Just as in an automobile both forward and reverse have different gearing. That was also true for the Fold equation. It took two separate programs that could not both be operating at the same time.

The oddity of the reverse equation was that once the Fold was back to its original start coordinate or zero start point, the equation kept going and operated on negative time. This is why he called it the Negative Fold Universe. He, however, had no understanding what the negative Fold equation represented.

The Earth that he had grown up on experienced time flowing from the point of the big bang that had created the universe out to infinity. He thought of it as flowing linearly from left to right.

He had not been able to determine how time was measured in the "Negative Fold Universe." He had now lost three bubble scouts and had no idea on how to retrieve them.

He was lost at how to maintain control of the bubbles entering the negative Fold zone.

He had come to the conclusion that he would need to personally go into the negative Fold realm to learn what was going on. He knew it was a risky thing to do but he felt that he would be able to figure out what was going on and make the adjustments that were needed to the negative Fold equation.

He had to try, and he had to do it alone.

This morning, he was carefully shaving and thinking about how he would handle the negative Fold universe and how to keep it invisible to the general population for the foreseeable future.

Negative Fold

He suddenly stopped and stroked his hair back and realized that he had a streak of grey hair along the right side. He muttered a silent curse. Growing old was one of the few things that had not crossed his mind. He wondered how, when he was doing multiple Folds, he could possible develop grey hair. The Fold process had been proven to transform a person from a most deformed state to a perfect body and it had let him get grey hair!

Pat entered and approached the second sink and saw Bram looking at his hair. She had meant to mention the grey to him but had been distracted by recent events and had forgotten. She reached up and let her fingers slide along the grey. She commented that it gave him the distinguished look of a wise man.

Bram smiled and thanked her and said that age unfortunately did not equate with wisdom.

He quietly finished shaving and let her know that he would be down getting a cup of coffee and then he was eager to get to work so he could tackle the conundrum of both wanting access to but wanting to keep everyone away from the negative Fold universe.

Pat spent a moment thinking up a ditty that the team could chant on the way into the work area compound. She smiled as she thought about the praise she had received about her ability to come up with good ditties, from Orlando, who was the master of coming up with ditties. He was the root of her current talent.

She thought for a few moments and thought she had a good one for this morning,

> *He's got a Silver streak, no he's not a freak*
> *He's growing old but growing bold*
> *I'm not too sure, It's what I am told*
> *Silver streak, no he's not a freak*
> *Growing old but growing bold*
> *Knows his way, through more than Fold*
> *Silver streak, no he's not a freak*
> *Growing old but growing bold*
> *Hi, Ho. Hi, Ho.*
> *No not growing old, just growing bold.*
> *Not too sure, it's what I'm told.*

She went to the kitchen for her coffee and enjoyed a slice of buttered toast with strawberry jam. She took a moment, jotted down the ditty, and handed it to Zoe letting her know that she should give it to Castor and Donna.

Zoe read the ditty and said she would be right back. She hustled down the stairs to the basement exit door and stepped out and handed Donna the ditty and said that they should use it this morning. She then returned to the kitchen just as Bram was rinsing out his cup.

Bram announced that it was time to go and led the way down the stairs to the basement exit.

When Castor and Donna said that they had a fresh ditty and took everyone through the first round, Bram smiled, he knew immediately who had written it. He looked at Pat and commented that she was getting as good as Orlando at writing ditties.

Zoe commented that Pat was better because she was closer and was able to ditty the most intimate occasions.

Pat laughed and said that she would limit her ditties to visually obvious things. The intimate parts were for her alone.

When Bram got to his office, Linda commented that for some reason he looked much more distinguished than she had previously noticed.

Bram smiled and shook his head and said she was looking much better than normal as well and wondered what make up she was wearing.

Linda smiled and said she declared a truce and asked if they should start with setting up his two-week work schedule.

Bram replied that he wanted fifteen minutes and then they could set up the next two weeks.

He went in and started the pot for hot water.

He was followed in by his two FBI bodyguards, Zoe, and Eric.

Zoe asked if he was going to have tea or coffee. She would get the coffee ready if that was his choice.

Bram thanked her and chose coffee.

He then went to the bookshelf and opened the little door leading to the two mice he had returned with from the desert where they had visited the rock where he had sat for more than a year during the development of his Fold equation.

He had gone there to visit Einstein his pet mouse who had been his advisor during the development of the Fold equation and whom he had returned to the boulder a few months before.

On this visit Einstein had given him two of his offspring that he had brought back the day before.

Pat had helped him name the two. One was Isaac, named after a famous scientist and the other, Ada, was named after another famous scientist. They both came out and got into his hand. Bram carried them to his desk and put them down at the center of the picture of the milky way. This picture was the size of his desk and was under the class covering. It was the picture that had captured his imagination when he was a young boy, and it had drawn him into the field that he was now pursuing.

He quietly told the two mice that he was going to ask for their help to set up the way to handle the negative universe the way that their father had helped him set up the Fold equation.

He smiled and pointed to them and said that they had both agreed by shaking their heads in the affirmative.

Zoe brought over his coffee and petted each of the mice with her finger and then put down some cookie crumbs.

Bram smiled and asked if she were trying to take his job or replace his relationship with his new advisors.

Zoe shook her head and said that she did not want a silver streak in her hair and that she would stick with dodging bullets and taking on the bad guys and he could go grey thinking about the Fold world.

Bram responded that he thought maybe the grey streak was a result of worrying about her tweaking his nose while he was deep in thought.

He then looked down to Isaac and Ada and told them that they now saw the stress he was constantly in because of this one bodyguard.

Eric brought over two more small cookie crumbs. He asked if the cookie was all that they got to eat.

Bram took Isaac and Ada back to the little door and they scurried in. He then opened the two doors below the main bookshelf and showed Eric the automated food and water set up that supplied the two mice with what they needed.

Isaac and Ada could be seen on the open side of the feeder taking a few nibbles.

He commented that the two had a fairly extensive tube system that also went outside where they could catch the morning sun.

He commented that there was even a transport tube that went to the Viewing Room and that it had been installed when the room was Zuri's office back when she needed the room for her wheelchair.

Eric said that he was impressed. He had wondered about Einstein and how he had lived while he was still with Bram.

Bram commented that he felt a little remorseful about having kept Einstein alone for so long. He said that Einstein had sent him a clear message by having him take two of his kids back with him.

He then smiled and said he hoped that the two were as smart as their father.

Zoe shook her head and said it was a little disconcerting to think that he was getting affirmation for his ideas from mice.

Bram smiled and said that he found the little creatures very critical to his thinking.

Linda knocked, entered, and said that his fifteen-minute reprieve was up, and it was time to work on his two-week work calendar.

Bram nodded and said that there was no escaping his responsibilities while she was around.

After spending almost an hour getting the next two weeks organized, Bram asked Linda to arrange for Marcus and Remi to meet with him. He suggested the ten o'clock open period on his calendar. He also asked her to see if Pat and Amy would be available for an afternoon trip to Mataia.

He asked Zoe and Eric if they needed to be with him on the Fold to Mataia.

Zoe commented that now that he had proven that he could get to the future it meant they could reach back into the past. This meant he needed more protection, not less.

Bram asked what she meant.

Zoe commented that unknown to any of them, he might have some enemy in the future that might take some sort of action against him. They should be ready for such an eventuality.

Bram nodded and then he smiled and said he agreed but he really felt that those in the future should love him and regard him as a scientific hero.

Zoe nodded and said that was exactly how everyone in their current time period should feel but it seemed that some of those that did not love him were willing to try to kill him.

Bram commented that they would need to rethink their current protection procedure and make sure they thought about an attack from some group from the future. He commented that they should put this discussion on the calendar and get General Tilson and Lacy in on the conversation.

Zoe suggested they do it sooner and not later because she had a bad feeling about the future.

Linda announce the arrival of Marcus and Remi, who walked in and welcomed him back from his trip to Gabon. Remi asked if they had ended up with a friendly new member on the Oversight Committee.

Bram commented that he felt great about the trip and about having an Oversight Committee that would be supportive overall of the Fold effort.

He then let them know that what he wanted to do now was to make the negative Fold capability invisible to the world for the foreseeable future. He wanted them to visit Mataia and determine what they needed to do to establish a center where everything about negative Fold would be located.

He wanted to set up a work center that was harder to get in or out of than Fort Knox. He made the point that the negative Fold capability was worth more than all the wealth of their world and when that became known they would all be in danger.

He pointed out that it also was the ying and yang of the world of the good and the bad. He shared what Zoe had said about not everyone loving him. He did not understand why that was the case but as she had pointed out he was not allowed to go anywhere without someone attacking him. She had challenged him and asked him if he thought everyone in the future would love him.

Remi looked at Zoe and commented that he had seen her in action and that Bram should listen to her carefully.

Bram said that he had listened and was going to review all the protection systems and protocols that they had set up and add the threat from the future as a new complication.

He said that he would have Linda set up a session with General Tilson and Lacy for the following day. He said that they should all plan to attend and bring their attack from the future scenarios to share.

Marcus commented that he was going to ask his kids about an attack from the future and how it would be carried out. He said that he would make it a game and see what they would come up with.

Bram said that sounded like a great idea. He then added, "from the mouths of babes."

He then took the two into the objective of the meeting and that focused on setting up the negative Fold work area on Mataia.

Marcus and Remi both agreed and threw in their ideas about the design of the work center.

When it came time for lunch, he called it quits, and they went to the cafeteria.

Amy and Pat were sitting together when they spotted Bram coming in for lunch. Pat commented that his protectors were all acting as if danger were close at hand. Amy looked around the sparsely populated cafeteria and said that she did not see any threats.

Pat knew that Zoe had commented that the threat level had risen, but she had not volunteered any information but had commented that she would soon have Bram working on better protection.

Bram walked over to Pat and said that he was looking forward to going to Mataia after lunch and was that something that could possibly be made to happen. He was about to go and get his lunch when Chef D'Carluca brought out a dish that he said he was perfecting that he called Swooshian Spaghetti di Mare and that he wanted to have Bram be the first to try it and give him feedback.

He looked around the table and asked if anyone else wanted to be a judge of his latest creation.

Everyone raised a hand.

He smiled. He commented that he had been counting on Bram making everyone hungry. He said that he would have the plates sent out.

Zoe commented that she was glad that she was on duty and that she would have hated to have missed out on one of the Chef's latest creations.

She commented that one of the benefits of guarding Bram was that he had exciting fishing trips that always seemed to feature fireworks, exciting vacations that had missiles and semi's trying to blow them up and a Chef that loved to try new dishes out on him.

Castor said that he had to fight off other Marines in order to keep his current assignment when they had found out he got to feast on Chef D'Carluca's special dishes.

Bram laughed and said that other than dealing with explosions and dodging lead, their work was a piece of cake.

Chef D'Carluca's Swooshian Spaghetti di Mare was a truly delicious spaghetti made with baby clams, mussels, squid, and shrimp in a thick dark blue sauce. He explained that the blue color came diluted from squid ink.

Everyone complimented him and said that once again he was pushing the limits of extremely great flavor.

After lunch Castor and Linda led the way to the hanger where the six-person Fold vehicle was waiting.

The Fold into the Mataia Arrival Terminal was uneventful.

Negative Fold

Bram described that he was looking to house the negative Fold effort as well as to house the vehicle or vehicles that would be limited to use in the negative Fold realm. He shared that he was planning on having a special vehicle that would hold ten with ten beds and a supply of food that would hold them for a month. He made the point that he was not planning any long forays into the negative Fold realm, but he was going to be prepared for any unplanned problem.

Pat looked at Amy and said that the empty hangar capable of holding Wheel One had plenty of space. She pointed out that a multilevel work center could be added. She said that the first level would be the Launch-Return site. They could equip that level with Sterile holding areas that would be isolated. The floor above it could hold a large lab. The third floor could be a large work center.

Amy commented that if the structure was located at the far end and the top two levels had windows to the external three sides they could make it feel very much like the work floor in the main Mataia Fold work building.

Bram asked Amy to walk off the area she was thinking about. After she had done this Bram asked to walk around the exterior of the hangar. He wanted to get a feel for the view, but he was also interested on how protection could be integrated into the building.

Once he had made the walk he asked Pat and Amy to join in on the meeting of Zoe, the General and Lacy to discuss how to make what they built as secure as his current office.

Amy thanked him and commented that she would take what she learned into consideration and have his office in the main Mataian building modified to have the same level of protection. She commented that protection had been overlooked when they built Einstein City and that she and Pat would take a cut at making sure they reviewed all the structures that Bram would frequent.

Bram thanked her and commented that every home and building should have a saferoom and they would need to experiment to see if they could set up a system that would prevent anyone from Folding into the safe rooms. He commented that making a Fold proof save room was going to be a challenge.

The next day during the meeting that focused on reviewing the safety protocol, Marcus said that his kids had come up with a variety of ideas that he would never have thought about.

One of their suggestions was to set up a laser screen around the perimeter of the room and test to see if Folding in was possible. They suggested that the laser screen should be similar to the screen on the porch screen door.

The second suggestion was to have a laser weapon that would sweep the room on a multilevel that was strong enough to cut someone into pieces.

He said another suggestion was to have a system that shot spikes up from the floor that were only inches apart.

The General laughed and asked what Marcus was feeding his kids.

Marcus said that he was always surprised by what his kids could come up with and that they were eating healthy meals.

Bram said that he would investigate each of their suggestions but the laser to cut people into pieces and shooting up spikes from the floor seemed to be out on the edge of what he had in mind.

He asked he General if he had any other better suggestions.

The General said, "touche" and then went on and suggested that they set up an armed bubble protection system on Mataia. He said he had two Marine's that needed to be promoted and who he did not want to lose. He could promote them and assign them to operate the protection bubble system on Mataia. They would still be housed on Earth, but they would always activate the bubble system on Mataia ahead of Bram and make sure the area was clear before his arrival.

Bram complemented the General and said that he thought that his suggestion should be implemented as soon as possible. He said that he would immediately begin to work on the laser screen suggestion that Marcus's children had made. He was thinking the screen should be a laser screen that as it sliced an object up would send each piece to separate random distances in negative space.

The General looked at Pat and asked what she was feeding Bram.

She smiled and said that Bram had the talent to take a simple idea and make it into a horror movie scene.

She then added that it was not what she was feeding him, but he was just seeing the side of Bram that she feared the most.

Amy joined in and commented that had she known about the Bram dark side she would have left him in the desert.

Bram stood up and bowed and said that he was ending the meeting on that note and planned to walk home slowly and absorb the painful feedback he had just received.

The General laughed and said he now knew how to quickly end meetings with him.

Chapter 2: Future Surprise

Bram began a head on attack to figure out how to gain control of the negative Fold universe. He knew that he needed to take an aggressive approach, and he needed to do it quickly before the Fold technology became known in his time. He read through several diverse fields dealing with the universe and reviewed competing theories. This led him to believe that the interaction of black matter, gravity, light, distance, and the expansion speed of the universe were all involved in creating the phenomena of a universe where time flowed both in a linear fashion from the big bang to infinity as well as the same universe where distance seemed to dictate the size of a rhombicosidodecahedron (RCID) where time was not measurable but inferred by the node sequence of the RCID. He was convinced that the greater the initial Fold distance the farther back in time the traveler would find themselves.

He personally had experienced that effect.

The way back from such a "time distance" was to jump from one RCID node to the next node in a given sequence for thousands, or perhaps millions of nodes. This in the linear universe he lived in would take an unmeasurable amount of time. He figured that most likely there was a way to choose what the next point on the RCID would be but currently he had no clue how to accomplish this.

As he reviewed the various papers that had been published on the measurement of distance across the universe and of the changing knowledge of how fast the universe was expanding the more convinced he was that the negative Fold environment was the result of the interactions happening similar to the interaction in his current time on the subatomic particle level. At that level, in the positive Fold world, it appeared that time did not exist. The negative Fold universe was a macro example of the same phenomena. Time did not exist in the negative Fold realm.

This was a concept that Bram found perplexing, but he figured that he would slowly work his way through until he understood the negative Fold universe. He likened it to the slow pace at which he had learned the Swooshian language.

He was convinced that what he had experienced in his first venture into the negative Fold universe was that distance had a similar attribute to time in his universe and he wondered if the measure of distance was linear from the big bang and followed the expansion speed of the universe.

The only thing that had saved him was the light that Pat had sent out with the old-fashioned Morse code that gave him a visual shortcut back to the time that he had entered the negative Fold realm. This meant that light was linear in the negative Fold realm and acted independently to both distance and time.

As he continued his studies it became apparent to him that the expansion of the Universe, the effects of gravity on light, the effects of gravity on matter and the fact that time did not exist, all interacted to produce a realm where reality was not the simple solid touch something and you knew it was real that was true in the positive Fold universe where time began with the big bang and existed as a constantly moving event.

He used the Bayesian inference statistical method and used all the elements he thought were pertinent to create a model of how nonexistent time affected where a negative Fold vehicle would end up. Once he had the model, he created a computer control program for one of the negative Fold bubbles.

He then needed to test how his Fold bubble moved in the negative Fold universe.

He engaged Marcus and together they began a series of trials and after several Fold trips they were able to recognize that the resulting location was based on the initial time settings in the Fold vessels control computer.

The time in the control settings seemed to interact with gravity and the black matter through which the Fold vessel traveled. Using his model, he reconstructed the gravity of the Universe throughout cosmic history in a computer model based on all the parameters including the positive Fold sections.

Bram realized that they were developing an equation that they could learn to manipulate not by brilliantly thinking through the model but by using plain old-fashioned trial and error experimentation. Each trial resulted in another increment of learning that allowed him to try yet another tweak of the model. This meant that he would be able to use his statistical model to continue tweaking the Fold equation and exploring the limits of traveling in the negative Fold realm.

Marcus commented that they were slow learners on how to handle how far the send journey would be and it was the light beacon that Pat had set up that allowed them to always retrieve the negative Fold vessel successfully.

Bram agreed and said that Pat had provided the practical tool that was going to allow them to slowly map the Negative Fold realm.

Both of them had been doing their work from their workspace in the new lab on Mataia as they waited for their new work area in the Mataia hangar to be built. Bram's bodyguards were with them at all times. Bram had made it a point that each day they Fold back to Earth for lunch.

Negative Fold

It was Zoe that noticed that Bram's grey streak had disappeared, and she commented that she had figured out why Bram had suggested Folding back for lunch.

Bram chuckled because he had not noticed the change until Zoe joked about it. He put it down to the positive side effect of Folding. His team all had a list of ailments that they no longer suffered. He knew that his first mouse Einstein was living much longer than any mouse he knew about.

He speculated that somewhere in the future a huckster would be selling Fold trips with the claim that it would heal any ailment. As he thought about it he knew that more experimentation on that side effects of Folding was needed.

Pat had taken the lead in the ultimate transformation that took Zuri from her wheelchair through a phenomenal body transformation. Zuri was currently nearing the end of her time attending Oxford. She had moved universities from the one that accepted her in her wheelchair and had gone to Oxford where no one knew she had been wheelchair bound for all her life. She was a Fold miracle.

Zoe observed Bram thinking and figured he had come up with yet another project. She had learned to read the moments when Bram hit on a new thought. She had never told him that he would close his eyes and when he opened them, smile, and nod to himself.

Bram realized that his protection team was waiting for him to disembark the Fold vehicle. He had been lost in envisioning how therapeutic Folds should be managed. He would ask Pat to take the lead and organize that area.

Pat sat at the table with Amy. They were both looking forward to the usual team lunch. They had just completed the entire structure that would be the Negative Fold work building on Mataia. The entire structure had been built on a slab next to the Fruit Barn Production area on Earth. It would be Folded into location by the end of the week. They needed to work with Marcus so they could Fold it into the precise location at the end of the hangar.

She and Amy had already removed the section of the hanger on Mataia that would be filled by the new section they had just finished. The final finishing touches would be done by the workers that were currently finishing the interior of the building. She was pleased with the openness of the building's negative Fold work area. She knew that Bram would spend a great deal of time there and she wanted it to be a comfortable place with an outstanding view.

She was aware that Bram had developed a very sophisticated laser barrier system based on the suggestion of Mylan and Marcus Jr.

Negative Fold

The grid to prevent any unsolicited Folds into the building would be implemented immediately after the building was moved into place. The shield was an amazing laser grid that would wrap around the entire building. Anything passing through it would be sliced into tiny pieces that were then randomly Folded into negative space. She knew that Bram had worked independently on the program and planned to locate the transmitter in a location only he knew about. It was his way of making it almost impossible for the future to interfere with the past.

She had the feeling that the transmitter would not be on Mataia but some undisclosed location and would have its own power system and would not need any attention.

She was aware that Bram had a Fold vehicle built that he was outfitting on his own. He let her know that no one would be allowed to see what was in it or to know where it was located. He said that it would also hold all the current knowledge of the Negative and the Positive Fold realms. He said that should he die, the information would be released a few centuries later.

She knew that he was trying to protect the entire human species as well as their Water World intelligent beings.

As Bram walked into the cafeteria, he looked over at where Pat and Amy were sitting and knew by their smiles that they had good news. He had been following the work they had been doing to get the Fold work center on Mataia built and knew they were close to completion.

He had purposely stayed away from the area where they were having it built. Instead, he had focused his efforts on setting up the anti-intruder laser grid.

He had recruited Erica to obtain a series of laser transmitters that could be set up to create a fly screen pattern around the entire work center. The power required to operated it was substantial and he worked with Remi to build a Fold vessel that would be able to generate the power needed and be able to keep the shield activated from a remote location.

He sat down and took a few bites of the slice of rare top loin roast that he was dipping in a sauce that Chef D'Carluca had insisted he try. The sliced fried green tomatoes were his effort at making sure he had a vegetable on his plate.

He looked at Amy and asked if she had crashed one of the Hilos.

She shook her head and asked why he would ask such a question.

He smiled and said that he observed that she was fidgeting and closely watching him eat.

Pat said that the two of them were excited to be able to announce that the negative Fold structure would be Folded into place on the following day and then they would have the structure activated three days later. He would then be able to activate his anti-intruder laser grid.

Bram complimented them at the speed at which they were setting up the structure and getting it into place. He said that he had focused on a much simpler effort and was lagging behind the timing they were achieving. He said that he would have to put the shield grid back on the front burner so that he could immediately activate it when they had the building in place

He added that he wanted to prevent the future from putting in any monitoring or spying devices. He wanted a clean work area.

Pat commented that she figured that he would be far ahead of any action the future might take.

Bram shook his head and replied that he was hoping that speed would at least keep him in the lead.

Zoe felt a shiver run down her back. She spoke softly to Eric and said that they should be prepared. Eric knew immediately that Zoe had experienced one of her intuitive moments and was now in an activated high adrenaline state. It was the same when they were getting on the car ferry on the trip through Norway.

She had the premonition then and her swift actions had saved them. The two of them had discussed these feelings she got and how they had always been accurate.

He had no idea what had caused her to feel that way, but he had come to know that she was correct one hundred percent of the time.

Eric excused himself and said he would return shortly. He left and went to a locker outside of Bram's office where they kept their Kevlar jackets and high-power weapons. He took all the weapons and protective equipment for all four of them out to the Fold craft. He laid the gear out for each of them and then returned to the cafeteria. He got there as Bram was getting ready to return to Mataia.

As he and Zoe got ready to take the lead back to the Fold vehicle, he let Thomas and Bob know that he had moved all their gear to the Fold craft, and they needed to be ready for action.

He then let Castor and Donna know they should be ready for action and did they need to stop anywhere to get their gear.

Castor shook his head, patted his backpack, and said they never went anywhere without their tools. He said that they were at full readiness.

Bram sensed that the atmosphere had changed. He likened it to the dip in atmospheric pressure just before a storm. He observed that his bodyguards were silent. When they got to the craft to get in each of his FBI bodyguards put on their Kevlar jackets and positioned their weapons at their seats.

Zoe handed him his vest and asked him to put it on. He did as she asked. He had his own weapon under his seat. He took it out, placed it and the extra ammo clip within reach as he sat down in the Fold vessel. He asked Zoe what was up.

He was not surprised that she simply replied, "premonition." This was the same as her reply to Matt when he had asked how she knew the truck in the tunnel was a trap and a bomb.

Remi and Marcus were both with him and it was clear to him that they had not picked up on the change in atmosphere. They were talking about the huge difficulty of figuring out the coordinates to place a building on a planet going through space and how Marcus had worked with Pat and Amy to place it exactly plus or minus one half inch within the rectangle represented by those coordinates.

Bram asked them to remain to the back of the team when they got to Mataia.

Their arrival to the Mataian Arrival-Departure Terminal was normal. Amy insisted on checking the terminal before allowing the rest of the team to disembark.

Their walk from the terminal up to Remi's lab was a little slower and Bram was surrounded by his bodyguards but otherwise it was uneventful.

Bram wondered if Zoe's intuition was off.

When they got to the lab door, Zoe put her open hand up and her finger of her other hand to her pursed lips. She then started a loud conversation with herself as she approached the door. She opened it fast and dove in toward the left and Eric followed and dove to the right. Castor and Linda dove straight in and slid on their stomachs with their back packs in front of them.

At first the silence made Bram think that Zoe had overreacted but then the continuous roar coming through the door seemed to be that of several large gatling guns firing simultaneously, and the area sounded like a full war zone. Thomas and Bob had pushed him to the wall and were trying to shielding him.

He pushed past them with his gun drawn and entered, turned to the right, and immediately shot two armed persons who were attacking his bodyguards from the side. The bodyguards had their attention toward their front and had not seen the attackers.

Bram continued along the wall firing at the attacking fighters. Then he took down two more when he was able to shoot behind the shields they were holding. He ran toward the other side of the room as he changed to a new bullet clip. He then fired from the side and shot the remaining fighters.

Once the shields fell, the barrage from Zoe, Eric, Castor, and Donna took down the wounded fighters.

He was glad that he had supported Zoe's anticipation of trouble and had put on his Kevlar vest because he had felt the hits as he crossed the room during the fight. He had been hit several times and was sure he would later feel the pain but at the moment his adrenaline was serving its purpose.

He watched as Zoe walked up to two wounded attackers and shot them. The grim look on her face warned him not to say a word. She checked to make sure the other attackers were dead. She commented that only dead assassins would be sent back to the future.

He noted that Eric had gathered the attackers' weapons and was putting then into one of the steel chests. He wondered why and was about to ask when a loud explosion caused the chest to lose its shape and look more like a stainless-steel sausage.

He asked Eric how he had known that the weapons would blow up.

Eric replied that he hadn't known but that he and Zoe had discussed what to expect if the future came back to attack them. They had agreed that the weapons would most likely self-destruct, so that the past could not gain knowledge about the future weapons technology.

They had also discussed the fact that in a conflict the future would expect to win and would come in a group they felt would be sufficient to quickly overcome their adversaries.

Bram suggested they search for a Fold vessel.

Zoe commented that it was not in their time but would potentially Fold in to pick up the attackers. She asked that they all stay close to the wall while she walked around and checked out the lab. She got down and glanced along the floor and on top of the larger worktables.

She pointed to the four chairs at each of the four tables and said that the attackers had sat on the stools with their weapons at the ready and shields besides them. She went to the largest open lab area and said that the Fold craft from the future had sat down, and the attackers had all gotten out, then the craft had Folded away.

She squatted down and pointed to one of the tiles that had some scuff marks on it and commented when they had the time, they would be able to match the scuff mark material to some of the boots on the attackers.

Bram asked Castor if he had any grenades with him. The lab was silent for a moment.

Then both Linda and Castor commented that they always carried several grenades with them.

Bram asked if they knew how to booby trap the bodies so that the future would receive a reply to their attack that they were probably not expecting.

He said that they as a team should not say another word about the attack so that the future would not know about the surprise they were about to get.

Zoe smiled and commented that how to behave was getting more complicated by the moment. She asked for everyone to help her get the bodies ready to take a trip to the future.

Bram watched as Castor placed his four grenades on four bodies and Donna did the same. It was clear to him that Castor had done it before in actual battle conditions and that Donna was watching Castor, so she placed and handled her grenades that same way.

Castor said that he would wire all of them together once they got them into their Fold vehicle. He would then attach the wire to the door. He explained the grenades would explode the moment the door was opened. He was not sure about the strength of the Fold vessel, but the open doorway would provide a way that he could launch a cloud of shrapnel. He looked around and asked if they had shrapnel that they could use.

Bram asked Remi what he had in the lab that they could gather to fill a container with, to put in the doorway.

Remi and Marcus went around opening drawers and cabinets and filling a trash can with a variety of metal lab tools and threw in glassware that broke. They carried back a large plastic trashcan full of the mix of glass and a variety of lab tools that included a set of knives and some tools that looked as if they belonged in a horror movie.

Zoe got everyone to stand against the wall while they waited for the Fold vessel from the future to appear.

Bram smiled when it Folded in. The vessel was still the same basic u-tube design that they were currently using. It made him wonder how close in the future his attackers were. He figured it might be close to his hundred-year Fold time capsule.

He watched as the team loaded the bodies and Castor and Linda worked together to wire all the grenades together.

He took a quick walk through the craft. He looked into the various packs and found several computer-looking devices. He did not recognize the brands but knew that the future was close enough that the technology was still recognizable. He handed the computers to Marcus and said they were souvenirs that he could study.

Marcus had been silent for the whole time, he said that he would love to fire them up and see what they would learn. He suggested that they should first figure out how to copy the memory. He said that they would most likely spend some time using the supercomputer to get past any passwords or whatever the lock to the computer would be.

Bram nodded and said they would all participate in breaking into the computers from the future.

Bram pointed to the forward single seat and said that it seemed to be the control or pilots seat. He noted what he took as the Fold button and suggested they put a weight over it that they could cause to fall and initiate the Fold back to the future.

Castor took a heavy piece of metal and put a set of folded paper matches to hold it up over the button. He said that they would have about thirty seconds after he lit the matches before the heavy piece of metal fell on the button.

Everyone got out and stood against the wall.

Castor lit the matches, closed the Fold craft's door got against the wall and when his count got to the word "thirty" the craft disappeared.

He said he would love to be able to see if their return gift caused the damage, he was hoping it would.

Bram commented that it might just be possible, but he still had some complicated analysis and experimenting that he would need to do. He let the team know that if it ever became possible to travel to the future, he would see about arranging such a Fold for all of them. He commented that until he was able to block the future, they should all standby for the attacks from the future versus the attacks during fishing.

Bram had overlooked that the attacks on the lake could just as well come from the future as well as from the current time.

Ron Mueller

<u>Chapter 3: Future Focus</u>

ˢram had multiple areas in the negative Fold environment that he was eager to explore. The future had been at the bottom of his list. He felt he should leave the temptation of looking at what was to happen to mankind should be left untouched. However, the attack had catapulted it to the number one position, and he put every moment into understanding how to maneuver in this negative time realm.

He studied the elements in his positive Fold portion of his equation and thought about how he controlled the forward motion along the timeline. In doing so he realized that he had not adjusted the equation to account for the fact that time acted differently in the negative Fold realm. In fact, in that realm, he realized that he should replace most of the time variables in his equations with distance variables. He knew that he had to create a distance variable that he could calibrate based on how it acted in the negative Fold realm.

Bram made his first cycle of adjustments in the negative Fold equation and then used negative distance numbers. He decided on a way to test the adjusted equation.

He sent out a bubble with a specific value. Had it register where it was by snapping a picture of the galaxy and the solar system. He then had the bubble home in on the light beacon and return with the pictures. He then matched the pictures to the time that the galaxy matched the picture of the galaxy in the picture.

It took him more than a thousand negative Folds of the bubble before he, using the supercomputer was able to refine the negative Fold equations to enable his use of distance. This gave him the ability to move through the negative Fold realm in a controlled manner similar to the ability he had in the positive world he lived in.

He then asked Remi to work with him in testing the ability for them to reach into the future. He wanted to reach forward and determine who had initiated the attack on him and how had that individual known about Mataia.

Remi was eager to take part. He asked how they were going to prove that they could do that.

Bram said that he was going to deliver flowers to the future.

Remi asked again how they would prove that they had delivered flowers to the future.

Bram told him to take his picture when he left and then take it again when he returned.

He would take one at the point of delivery and then they could compare the result.

Negative Fold

Bram said that he would deliver flowers to Linda fifteen minutes into the future. He would have her take a picture of he, the flowers standing before her and behind him he would have the Fold vessel with the mechanical clock facing the picture. Her phone would record the time that the picture was taken and anything the two of them said would also be recorded.

He would return and Remi would take his picture again. They would then slowly walk to her desk and ask Linda how she liked her flowers and how long it had been since he had given them to her.

She should be able to show them the pictures she had taken of him that gave the time of delivery and Remi would have a picture of the time he had left to deliver the flowers and the time of his return. The pictures would verify the ability to interact directly with the future.

Bram shook his head as he commented about the inherent danger of anyone being able to do so. It was a power that if used improperly would threaten the very fabric of mankind's existence.

He then said, "let's do it."

Bram stepped into the two-person negative Fold vehicle with the flowers.

On his return Remi took his picture. They then walked slowly up to Linda's desk.

Linda's eyes widened when she was asked when the flowers had been delivered. She instinctively knew that she was being used to prove one of Bram's theories. She commented that she felt like a guinea pig. She replied that he should know but she had a picture of his delivery.

Bram asked her to print the picture. It printed with a date and time on the bottom of the paper.

Bram showed the picture to Remi. The Fold craft was in the picture and the large clock in view in the craft and the time on the picture from the phone were fifteen minutes different with Linda's phone time fifteen minutes ahead of the one in the craft.

Bram then had Remi show the pictures he had taken that were fifteen minutes and thirteen minutes earlier than Linda's time.

Linda smiled and complemented Bram on having discovered yet another great capability of the Fold equation he had developed, and she would enjoy flower deliveries whenever he wanted to deliver them from the past. She said that she needed to sit down as she absorbed how old he seemed to be now that she had interact with his much younger self a few moments before.

Bram nodded and said that he felt that now the Stetson family would have to be defending him from two fronts. The current groups that kept attacking him when they went fishing and those in the future who would most likely be attacking in some other fashion.

He did not say anything about the attack that the future had already carried out. He figured that he had to remedy that situation quickly and quietly.

Bram invited Linda to lunch and the three of them walked toward the cafeteria.

Pat and Amy were both waiting for him and once again smiling.

He stopped and got a bottle of sparkling water and a pint of Black Raspberry and Chocolate chip ice cream. He took off the lid and after his first spoon full, he asked Amy what she was smiling about.

Amy said that after lunch she and Pat were going to put the new building into position on Mataia.

Bram complemented them on their fast work. He commented that he would be able to put in the screen shield as soon as they had it in place. He remined them that the building needed to have a one-foot void below it to accommodate the laser screen.

Pat said that the building had been poured with feet that were one foot high. When they put it down at the coordinates they had given to Marcus, the building would be his to protect.

Bram commented that he wanted all the buildings on Mataia to have the protective envelop that the new work center would have.

Pat nodded and commented that he had just given she and Amy an assignment that would be a challenge, but they would figure it out. She asked if the protection was necessary.

Bram nodded and said that they really had no choice. The future had already made the first move and most likely would continue until he could figure out how to neutralize that situation.

Pat used her spoon to take a taste of his ice cream and asked what he was celebrating.

Bram replied that they would all soon know but at the moment he could not share that information.

Linda said that she thought he was celebrating being nice to her and giving her flowers.

Bram nodded and said that Linda was right. The flower delivery had made him happy.

Remi said he was just happy to be able to enjoy a great lunch with a great group of people. This was his way to deflect any question that might come his way. He was trying to shield himself from being asked about what was up. He was terrible at making up deflecting stories.

Bram commented that as soon as the building was Folded into place, he would enclose it in the laser screen grid that Marcus's kids had suggested.

He looked at Marcus and said that on Sunday they should have breakfast so they could show the kids how their idea had been implemented and how it would protect all the buildings on Mataia.

Marcus said that would be great. He shared that he had not let the kids know that their suggestion had been turned into reality. He said that he was sure that the two of them would be celebrating for weeks to come because they had asked him if their ideas had been accepted.

Bram said that so far their screen laser idea was the only idea that he had figured out how to use. He had added a few twists so that the future would find it very hard to figure out about the screen and how it functioned.

He didn't say anything, but he figured that the future had found out about Mataia some one hundred years in the future. That was the time frame he had used to have his information bubble appear. He now planned to go back in time and change that to one thousand years. He wondered how he would recognize how his actions might have changed history.

He would have to determine some marker that he could reliably use to determine what had changed.

Remi led the way back to the hangar where two-Fold vehicles were sitting. One was loaded with a huge battery system and a computer system that controlled multiple laser transmitters and random transmit controllers that were situated around Mataia. The transmitters had multiple backups and would be able to sustain a laser intrusion protection envelope around every building on Mataia.

Remi pointed out that protective bubble systems and multiple backups and that the backups would be randomly located at coordinates that would also change randomly. He shared that the supercomputer predicted that the probability of someone finding and eliminating a protective bubble would be expressed by one divided by a number larger than one trillion.

Bram made the last adjustments to the control vehicle and then launched the control vehicle out to the coordinates he had determined was optimum for its purpose.

He asked Remi to prepare the second vehicle and position it at a random coordinate and now that he had brought up the fact that the laser bubbles had triple backup, they should add a third control vehicle.

He then had Remi Fold all the control bubbles into position. The bubbles would also control the random particle transmit signals of the very small particles that would result from any attempted entry.

They worked on it for the rest of the day and toward the very end of the day, Pat and Amy let them know that the building was in place and his to control.

Bram immediately activated the laser screen system and all the backup systems as well.

He thought about all the events that had transpired on one very long day.

He realized that he was beyond being exhausted, he was ready to collapse.

His trip home, laying down in his bed was a unanswered mystery when he got up. He went into the bathroom and automatically began brushing his teeth. Then he looked in the mirror and was just realizing that he had been hit multiple times during the gun battle when Pat walked in.

She looked over at him and just stared at the bruise marks on Bram's chest, his arm and left side. She counted at least ten bruises maybe more because some seemed to be double hits. She was shocked and asked what he had not told her about his morning on Mataia the day before.

Bram leaned in close and whispered that he feared the future was listening. They had sent back an assassination squad that the FBI team members with the help of the Marine team members had taken out.

Pat whispered back that evidently, he had taken an active part in the fight as well.

Bram nodded and replied that they had been outnumbered and needed his help. He had not realized how many times he had been hit until this morning.

He let her know that her quick work would allow him in the future to be enclosed in a protected work environment.

Pat asked if he was planning on an easy day.

Bram nodded and said that he wanted to spend the morning in his office and the afternoon at the rec center.

Pat gave him a gentle hug and said that she would shadow him. She said that she wanted to make sure the future did not reach out for him until he developed the defensive weapons with teeth that he needed.

Bram thanked her and let her know that his defensive weapons would all have extremely sharp teeth and a bite that would be lethal.

He spent the rest of the morning thinking through how he could protect the people around him from the future and how to still let the world benefit from the Fold capability.

He wished the oversight committee had supporters that would guide the deployment of the positive Fold capability. He was not confident that would happen in the current political environment of the world. He would see how that might happen.

What gave him more concern was how he would handle the ability that the negative Fold would give that same group of people to act against the past or conversely would allow those living in his time the ability to reach into the future to change what was to happen.

He decided he would ask his team to guide him in determining how to handle both matters.

He figured that he should take the rest of the day to recover and to relax at the rec center. After breakfast he and his entourage went down to the rec center.

He was stiff as a board and lost at ping-pong and at pool.

It was clear to Zoe that he was not his usual competitive self and did not have his smooth moves. She had seen Bram during the gun battle and figured that he had been hit. She walked up to him and asked how many times he had been hit.

Bram quietly replied that somewhere between six and twelve times.

Zoe's eyes went wide and said that he had not said one word about it and had worked for the rest of the day.

Bram said that he did not want the future to know that they had almost succeeded in their effort to kill him. If they realized that, they might immediately try a second time. He said he needed time to effectively neutralize the future.

Zoe said she was on the side of taking direct action against the future by attacking them and eliminate that threat.

Bram said that on Monday they would go to the future and deliver a message that would make it clear that acting against the past had an expensive bite to it.

Zoe smiled and said that his protection team members would all be ready to deliver the message.

Bram smiled and told her to ask Linda and Castor to bring plenty of C4 with them.

Pat watched Bram's quiet interchange with Zoe and noted her smile as she walked away. She knew that Bram had told her about his bruises and that he probably had told Zoe that he had a payback idea in mind. That was the only explanation to the smile on Zoe's face.

Pat saw her walk over to Eric and then the two then walk over to where Castor, Diane, Mike, and Bob were sitting and quietly enjoying their drinks. She watched the group talking and then they all did a fist victory pump in the air.

She figured the future was in for a surprise that the past would deliver in a spectacular display of force. She knew that Bram would reply with enough force that the future would not be able to ignore the message.

Bram walked over and said that he was ready to go back to the house and relax in his office, but he needed to have someone to sit with on the two-person couch and keep him warm.

Pat smiled and raised her fist and did a victory pump and said that she was ready for a good book.

She watched as the protection group responded in kind. She knew that she and the group were celebrating two very different scenarios, but both had to do with Bram as the center.

On the way to the house Bram asked Eric to have the team scan the house for listening devices or anything that might be out of the ordinary.

Castor said that he and Diane would check the outside area around the house as well.

Bram thanked him and said that for the next few days until they had set up the laser intrusion net around their work areas at their Earth Fold compound, they would need to be extra cautious.

He added that a rapid response to the future needed to occur so it would know that they were not safe just because they were in the future. Those in the future had to realize that they were vulnerable too.

Zoe had Bram wait outside until a sweep of the house could be made. After about twenty minutes she returned with several listening devices and two devices that appeared to be cameras. She asked Bram how he knew the house would be bugged.

Bram smiled and said that he had no idea but figured that such action could easily be taken by someone who was monitoring what the past was doing. He said they had spent enough time at the rec center for the planting of the devices to occur.

He held a descriptive finger in the air and loudly said that the future should take a hike.

Castor used a more descriptive action with an arm motion, a slap on his muscle and a Bafungo!

He handed Zoe several similar listening devices and cameras. He said he had called in a group of Marines to do a more thorough search around the outside of the house.

Bram said it was late and suggested they go in and enjoy the evening and then get ready for a great Sunday morning breakfast.

Ron Mueller

Chapter 4: Pomp and Circumstance

Sunday morning breakfast at the Bram home was known as the breakfast of surprises and the breakfast of friends. It was a breakfast that everyone liked to be invited to. Everyone knew that it was a time when Bram seemed to share many of his ideas or to highlight the people doing something doing some interesting work.

He worked hard at making each Sunday morning breakfast a highlight that those getting an invite celebrated. None of those being invited could be given the official or the national recognition that they deserved because the Fold program remained a super top-secret project. But he wanted those around him to feel valued, to be recognized and to see that their efforts were making a positive difference.

At work, on a daily basis, he made his rounds, and he made it a point to praise everyone for the work they were doing.

Sunday breakfast was a day when he could put a few of them on center stage and shine the spotlight on them.

This morning, he was going to highlight the fact that two of their young members had suggested the means that he had used to create the system that would provide intrusion protection from the future and also protect them from those in their own present time.

He would share the enhancements that he had added because of the suggestion Marcus's two children had made and then see if they had any other suggestions they might want to add.

He had spent Saturday afternoon using a scout bubble that he Folded to Mataia. He methodically took pictures of the new work center that Pat and Amy had Folded into place on the previous day. He was impressed at how the new building section seemed to have been constructed at the same time as the hanger. Once he had taken pictures from inside and outside of the hangar and had panned the landscape that would be viewed out of the third-floor work center windows, he was ready to demonstrate the protective screen that surrounded the building.

He had added the protective screen mere moments after the new section had been put into position. It was invisible to the eye, but it was fully operational.

He positioned his picture taking bubble scout high in the hangar and then Folded a second empty bubble to the coordinates in the center of the negative Fold lab area. His picture taking scout bubble captured the flash when the empty bubble hit the laser protective screen.

Negative Fold

The laser web was visible during the few seconds that the bubble was being destroyed by the laser screen and the small sections were sent to random coordinates in negative space.

He originally had the idea to visually simulate the laser screen but instead had decided to slow down the actual impact of the incoming bubble by a factor of ten thousand. The impact appeared as a slowly growing spot until it was the diameter of the sphere and then it slowly shrank back as the bubble passed its widest point then shrank to nothing at which time the laser field again became invisible.

He was intrigued by the tiny sparkles that appeared when the bubble shredded material that the shield Folded into negative space. It seemed that different Fold distances created different colors. The resulting sparkles made the sequence look similar to a fourth of July fireworks starburst that was occurring in slow motion.

He smiled as he looked at the result and knew that he had a unique video, and that the sparkling highlighted new information that needed to be studied. He knew who he would ask to study if the Fold color was associated with a negative Fold distance. He wondered if the light color spectrum could be used to map the negative Fold distances and be correlated to time.

Perhaps each node of the RCID decahedron had a color or color spectrum similar to a barcode. If so the RCID decahedron could then be mapped and perhaps it would allow a bubble to go directly to the desired node and bypass the rest of the nodes by sending it to a specific color bar code. This would then allow rapid negative Fold coordinates to be programed and the time that a cycle took could be managed using computer control.

This would result in the positive and negative Fold environments being controlled in the way that humans were used to using time as a control variable.

He made a final improvement to the video by adding music to the background and added a few comments to some of the video sections.

He let Pat know that he was excited about showing what he had accomplished.

Pat knew that Bram always enjoyed Sunday morning interactions with those he now considered their friends. The associations of the Fold community were numerous, and everyone was close. She had watched Bram develop almost every member in the community. He was relentless in encouraging individuals to be engaged with those around them in a positive way.

He did not push people to interact. He pushed people to learn from each other. He pushed them to recognize, accept and value differences. He pushed them all to respect each other and treat others as they wished to be treated.

She had talked with Amy about the fact that Bram enjoyed recognizing and rewarding those around them and that he was planning to award both Marcus Jr. and Mylan scholarships to any university they chose. He had shared the fact that the two had come up with the best defense against intrusions that might come from any time frame.

Amy smiled and said that she had close and deep experience with Bram's ability to inspire. He had inspired her to try to apply for a seat in the class of Astronaut training where the two of them had met, and he had also made sure that she got a seat. She commented that when Bram focused his mind on an objective he always achieved it.

She gave a small laugh and said that she had brought Pat back as her reward for him. She complemented Pat on having beat out a mouse named Einstein to be Bram's soul mate.

Pat laughed and joked that he should have left Amy flying hilo's in the desert.

The two took their coffee and joined Bram at the table and asked how he planned to engage his two special guests.

He replied that he was going to use the building that the two of them had just finished putting in place on Mataia and demonstrate an actual attempted intrusion.

Pat showed and voiced surprised because he had not given her any warning about an actual demonstration. She and Amy had turned over the building on Mataia to him late on Friday and now he was ready to demo his protective system. She asked when he had the found the time to prepare such a demonstration.

Bram confessed to having discussed it with Remi while at the rec center. He had asked Remi to provide him with two bubbles. When he came back to his office he had spent a couple of hours in the afternoon to try out the defense system.

Pat commented to Amy that living with Bram was to live in a double fast forward supercharged mode and there was no getting off the train because it made no stops.

Amy laughed and said that she should have warned Pat about the Bram train, but she wanted her to meet him first, after they had made it through their astronaut training. They had both recognized that the Bram train was the best opportunity they would ever get. She then said that she had witnessed Pat willingly get on the special cabin on the train and she should not complain about no getting off opportunities.

Zoe commented that fast forward seemed to keep all of his protection team on their toes and made each a day an exciting experience.

Castor commented that fast forward provided plenty of active weapon field experience.

Donna smiled, nodded, and added, "And some."

The doorbell rang and Zoe and Eric went to the door and checked who was ringing it.

Zoe opened the door to let Marcus, Marcus Jr and Mylan in. She saw that Remi was with them as were Linda, Lacy, and Ray. They all entered and Zoe led them to the kitchen to get their breakfast and drinks.

A few moments later Erica and Gerry, General Tilman and his attaché Matt were at the door. Once they were let in they went to the kitchen, got their breakfast, and sat down.

Amy commented to Pat that Erica was the top example of how Bram turned a lemon not into lemonade but into a sweet strawberry smoothie. She commented that Bram did not bring enemies close to his chest but instead made them friends who realized that life could have sunshine and happiness associated with it.

Pat replied that Bram considered Erica one of their best friends. And she made the point that the two of them knew how effective she had been at filling all their requests. She had become the lever and fulcrum that had made raising Einstein City from the ground up possible. She added that Bram's presentation after breakfast was only possible because Erica had been able to round up the required materials for the new Negative Fold Center at lighting speed.

Erica smiled raised her cup of tea and said that she had excellent hearing and agreed with everything that Pat had said.

Amy nodded raised her cup and silently mouthed a "thank you."

Bram had been quietly watching everyone. He had also overheard most of Pat's and Amy's verbal exchange and liked the way the two of them had complimented Erica.

He announced that this was a special breakfast and that he had designated it "The Young Geniuses" breakfast.

He pointed at Mylan, and Marcus Jr and said that they were what made this breakfast special.

He was a little surprised when the room went silent. He then said they should all enjoy what he was going to share and suggested everyone refill their drinks and asked that the donuts and sweet rolls that Ted had delivered be put out on the table.

Thomas brought them out on three platters. He and Bob strategically placed them so everyone could reach them.

When the room was again settled, and everyone had what they wanted Bram turned on the large viewing screen. The low background music of pomp and circumstance provided the introduction. He had added all the names of those present and had highlighted the contributions each had made.

He had made the golden yellow contribution writing scroll slowly up the screen and back over stars and galaxies in the dark background. It was a ploy used by many movies to highlight the central theme of a movie.

He momentarily stopped that video and congratulated everyone for their great work and asked for a round of applause. It seemed that the Marines did not know how to clap but every one of them shouted out "Hurrah" multiple times during the applause.

Bram smiled and pumped his fist in the air and closed with a "Hurrah."

He then thanked Marcus Jr. and Mylan for providing the answer of how to protect everyone from those who lived in any time and who wanted to break into their facilities and homes. He let them know that their laser idea was the only protection suggestion that had so far been implemented.

He then reactivated the video that took everyone on a tour of the new Negative Fold Facility.

He complimented Amy, Pat, Marcus, and Erica for having set a record pace in getting the facility built, the offices and work areas be beautifully appointed, and the building placed in the ware house in a manner that it seemed to have been part of the original construction.

Then he took them on a brief external tour that highlighted the view of the mountains, and the sea.

The tour entered the building and highlighted the dining room and break areas and the storage, refrigeration and the kitchen that had been designed by Chef D'Carluca.

It then went up to the second floor to the Fold Lab, the computer center, a machine shop, and the work area.

Remi commented that Pat and Amy had delivered his dream lab.

When the tour entered the third-floor office and work area everyone commented that they wanted to work there. The camera slowly panned the room and showed the finished interior, the furniture, and the artwork. Everyone made a comment about the view and the striking layout and about the appointment of the work area that had been done.

Pat pointed at Erica and said that the appointment was totally her doing. She added that the view was Mataia, and it was Amy that had insisted on having surrounding glass walls as the design of that floor.

Bram pointed to Erica and thanked her for the great furniture and pictures that she had selected and delivered in record time.

He then pointed to Amy and Pat and complimented them on their ability to build and place the beautiful three-story building with an awesome view in less than a month. He commented that the two of them could make a fortune in building homes back on Earth.

He looked at them with a sad look and commented that they had a whole Fold community of buildings that required an upgrade.

He stopped the video and let Amy, Pat and Erica know that he had requested Jeffrey to award a bonus to each of them for their exceptional contributions.

Amy thanked him and commented that she was once again glad that she had picked him up in the desert.

Erica said that she had made a personally right decision in accepting the role of managing the Dalles based Fold organization, and she planned to live her wonderful life with her trophy husband and travel the world spending her bonus money.

Pat thanked him and said she just wanted to be able to sit on their couch and read books while leaning against him and she planned to give her bonus to whatever charity Linda recommended.

Amy said, "Wow, I can't look like a cheap skate so now I will have to do the same with my award."

Erica shook her head and said that she was not sure what the award amount would be, but she planned to keep enough for at least a couple of vacations, but she would join both Pat and Amy in channeling the award to the organization that Linda recommended.

Linda smile and thanked them for being generous and said that she would work with the three of them and together they could determine which organization they wanted to enrich.

Bram had waited quietly during the exchange. He then he said that everyone was doing great work and all deserved recognition and that he would take the opportunity to see that no one felt left out.

He then said that one suggestion made by the two youngest folks at the table, Mylan, and Marcus Jr. was the only one that had resulted in the creation of a Fold defense system for all the Fold community homes and work buildings.

He then again showed the negative Fold facility. He said that it was currently shielded by a laser grid with holes that were the same size as the holes found on most normal screen doors.

Bram asked the two if what he was describing was what they had suggested.

Mylan nodded and said that it was exactly what she and Marcus Jr. had talked about.

Bram then said that he had added a couple of special features. He pointed out that the lasers were powerful enough to slice up almost all objects that might try to penetrate it. He said that he had used an actual empty bubble that Remi had provided and set its destination Fold coordinates to the center of the lab.

On the video, a small bubble came slowly into view. Bram explained that he had slowed down the picture by a factor of ten thousand, so they were watching everything in extremely slow motion.

The bubble encountered the laser screen and the small laser squares appeared as a circle of sparkling lights that slowly shot fire of different colors into the air.

The sparkling circle first grew in size and then slowly began to shrink. Finally, the sparkling stopped, and the building looked like any other building. There was no indication of anything unusual about the building.

He then shared that the enhancement that he had added sent each tiny fragments of the object interacting with the laser screen randomly out into the negative Fold universe. Each piece created a sparkle of a different color.

He looked at Marcus and said the sparklers were the result of his children's idea and that it was going to be his job to figure out what the sparkling lights meant.

The picture went black and then after a quiet moment and a drum roll, "Pomp and Circumstance" came more loudly through the speakers. As it played he announced that for suggesting the laser screen protective shield idea he had set up the Mylan and Marcus Jr. scholarship fund that would pay the expenses to any college they chose, and they would each immediately get a five-thousand-dollar gift from the Fold program.

Mylan smiled, said thank you, and then she said that she would put half of the five thousand in her savings account, but she said she wanted to spend the other half on all the weekend vacations that she could get her dad to take.

Marcus Jr. said he would do the same.

Marcus smiled and said that he was very proud of his two kids, and he would plan on taking every weekend Fold vacation that he could schedule. He thanked Bram for the scholarships and said that he saw sparkling lights in his future.

Bram then shared that he was naming the protective screen the "MyMar Shredding Screen (MMSS)" after them and that a screen would soon encompass all of their living and work areas as well as all the vacation homes and apartments on both worlds.

He then challenged Mylan and Marcus Jr. to play a ping-pong game against the current doubles champions and he wanted to play each of them in a game of snooker.

Pat knew that Bram was the best ping-pong player as well as the best snooker player. She was sure he had asked Zoe and Eric, who were the doubles champions, to play Mylan and Marcus Jr. because his bruises were affecting him, and snooker was a game that he knew how to loose when he chose to.

Linda volunteered to call her parents and ask them to cater an afternoon grill out at the recreation center.

Bram agreed and said that the grill out would begin at the time that the first brats were on the grill.

He said breakfast was over, but everyone should stay as long as they wanted and enjoy donuts and drinks until it was time to go to the grill out.

He excused himself and said that he was going to his office to relax before having to face the competition he expected to face on the snooker table.

He was feeling the effect of all the bullet hits he had taken and just wanted to sit down on his recliner and let his body chill.

Later, when Linda called and let Pat know that her father had just thrown the brats on the grill she and the rest went down to the recreation center.

Word about the grill out had circulated and the number of people that began to show up seemed to be skyrocketing. It appeared that everyone was going to show up.

Bram let Ted know that everyone was welcome to take part and enjoy the food. Ted nodded and put some additional brats and dogs on the grill. He called out to Rita to bring some more ribs.

Bram watched as Mylan and Marcus Jr. played a game of ping-pong with Zoe and Eric. She and Eric let Mylan and Marcus Jr run up the score then Zoe demonstrated her skill with a series of trick shots that closed the margin but when she was within a couple of points she began to miss. Mylan and Marcus Jr. got to eleven exactly two points ahead and won the game.

Linda brought two plates with a barbequed rib and a prepared hot dog loaded in what she called a Chicago dog and asked the two what they wanted to drink with their late lunch.

Bram was sitting at the table with the two and asked if either of them had ever played snooker.

Marcus Jr. said that neither of them had ever played.

Bram then suggested that he would teach them how to play instead of making it a contest.

Mylan said that would be great since she had wondered what the larger table was all about.

He then shared a bit of Snooker history and made the point that it was a more sophisticated and skill-based game than pool. He pointed at the Snooker table and then pointed at the Pool table and asked if they could see how much larger the Snooker table was. He said that Snooker was much more difficult than pool because there were many more shots, many more strategies and many more positions as compared to the game of pool.

He explained that the game was invented in Jabalpur India by a British army officer, Sir Neville Chamberlin. At that time, the word "snooker" was a well-established derogatory term used to describe inexperienced or first-year military personnel and somehow it was the name given to the game.

Bram then put on a demonstration of the different shots that could be made and he had Mylan and Marcus Jr. try a few. In a few moments it became clear that Mylan had enough of snooker, but Marcus Jr. seemed to like the game.

Bram commented that Jabalpur, India was just about 100 miles from Agra where the Taj Mahal was located. He let the two know that Melisa had established a vacation apartment in Agra that was available for a Fold weekend vacation.

He suggested that Mylan visit the Taj and see the Red Fort and they could then all drive down to Jabalpur and visit the museum that had one of the original snooker tables on display.

Pat commented that she was not sure that Marcus's two would want to do that weekend vacation, but Bram's story had convinced her that she wanted to spend a weekend at Agra.

Mylan asked if maybe the five of them could go together on the next available weekend.

Bram asked Marcus whether that would be acceptable and that reminded him that there would also be bodyguards coming along.

Marcus agreed that it would make it a great Fold weekend.

Ron Mueller

Chapter 5: Forward Payment Plan

The impromptu grill out was the medicine that Bram had needed. The next morning, his bruised chest, the bruises on his left arm and left side were still tender but the yellowish, blue, and purple made the bruises on his body look worse than they had at first. He wondered how long it would take before they disappeared.

Pat wondered how Bram was feeling but she figured his work would keep him from focusing in on what she knew had to be painful bruises. She lightly touched his bruises and then told him that he looked like a person that had been beat up by the mafia for not paying off his gambling debt.

Bram smiled and said that she had the right metaphor and that he did owe somebody payment and he was going to pay it back.

The jog in to work actually helped him by loosening up the ab and arm muscles. He asked his bodyguards to accompany him to the viewing room.

They were greeted by Marcus and Remi.

He asked everyone to sit down so they could spend the early morning planning how to repay the future for trying to kill them.

Zoe smiled and said that they were only trying to kill him, and his bodyguards were just seen as collateral damage.

Bram asked that the Viewing room get checked for any listening and visual recording devices.

A few moments later Zoe declared it clear.

Bram explained that he wanted to demonstrate to the leaders of the group from the future that had attacked them that they too were vulnerable. He planned to totally demolish their office or work center. He hoped to be able to take the building down but to do it at night with the building empty. He had no desire to hurt any incidental people that had chosen to work all night.

Bram then said that he was going to write on the white board and once they had a plan agreed to he would wipe it clean. He said that from now on information would need to be doubly protected.

He then listed what he thought they would need to do and asked the team to identify any misses.

He said that they would need to send out a series of scout bubbles to identify the time in the future that would be the point of their forward payment.

Negative Fold

Marcus suggested that they use all thirty of their scout bubbles and position them five years apart. That way they could check one hundred fifty years in a few seconds. Then the gathered data could be processed in their supercomputer and by lunch time they should have the exact year in the future that they desired.

Remi pointed out that Earth was a loud planet that broadcast information out into space. The bubbles could be kept behind the moon and get all the information that the team needed. They would be there only a few seconds and would most likely never be sensed.

Bram had been writing down the logical order of what they needed. He said that once they found the year they were after, they would need to locate the headquarters of the group that attacked them.

Zoe asked how Bram planned to determine what the start time in the future where they should start the search.

Bram said that the computers carried by their attackers that he had in his possession had manufacture dates on them. He suggested that Marcus start at that date with the first scout bubble and then move forward in his suggested five-year increments.

Zoe said they should be able to identify the exact year and location by scanning the news for a report of an explosion that happened when they sent back the booby-trapped Fold vehicle with the dead bodies of the attackers. She figured that it would be reported as a gas leak or a lab explosion.

The location would allow them to then get drawings from the county computer records and they then would know the design of the building.

Remi said that once again this could be done by using a scout bubble as the relay station for the transaction between their supercomputer and the one at the county records office that held the building plans.

Castor said that while they were getting all the information together, he would contact a friend who had been in his unit that had gone into the business of demolishing buildings. He would get a quick lesson on what they should consider.

Bram suggested that once they had the building drawing, Castor share the drawing with his friend and ask him to recommend the optimum way to bring it straight down. He asked Castor to offer his friend payment for the information.

He looked at Marcus and said that once they had picked the year, he wanted to arrive at the building at midnight on a moonless night. He asked Marcus to determine the coordinates that would put their Fold transport inside the basement of the building.

Remi suggested that they verify the coordinates in the basement with a scout bubble and if it was on target and the area clear they would Fold in.

Bram suggested that after the verification they take a two-person Fold vehicle in first and make sure the larger one would fit. He did not want to Fold in with a load of C4 and accidentally be part of a huge explosion in the basement.

After rigging the building, they would Fold out to the coordinates of the home of the leader of the group that had attacked them and leave him a calling card.

Eric asked what the calling card would be.

Bram said that they would leave an unarmed chunk of C4 and a piece of chocolate in the kitchen with the message, "the past can be sweet" or it can be aggressive and much meaner" and that the past had the means to retaliate. The C4 would be placed in front of a family picture. The message would make the point that the building had been a warning but any future attempt to hurt someone in the past would result in a response that would sow mayhem into his personal world, and anyone associated with him.

Diane asked if he worried about starting a time war.

Bram replied that it had already started. His next step was to go back in time and change the time of Folding all the information about the Fold program from a one-hundred-year reappearance time frame which was where they were going, to a one-thousand-year time frame. He would Fold to that future to verify that it was a better time frame and if it was not he would go out farther in time.

Eric suggested that they needed to set up the study of the future and determine how they could influence the development of a society based on good versus the current one of conflict for power. He pointed to the fact that there might be bad people one thousand years or even ten thousand years in the future that might take the same action. He suggested that the Fold information be put on a long journey and that Bram figure out how to pass along the information of where the Fold information was located.

Bram said that Eric had a very good idea, and they would need to work fast before the Fold process became exposed in their time and became an issue that made the conflict worse. He had no idea how to move human nature from the desire for power and dominance to one of peace and love.

He said that he would need to rethink how to ensure that the Fold discovery moved into a peaceful future.

He said he would need to think about the best way to protect humanity from itself.

Marcus picked coordinates that started their search and sent the thirty scouts out on five-year increments. He commented that without their supercomputer and the program he had just written it would be impossible to identify the coordinates of a location from behind the moon. He hoped that his bubbles were remaining invisible and that in the five seconds each spent in their future time frame they went undetected or if detected became observations that had no explanation.

Zoe, Eric, Thomas, and Bob were doing rapid analysis of the returned data.

Diane and Castor had contacted the friend and were becoming proficient in the process of bringing a building down. Castor offered to pay his friend for consulting with them and setting up a building for demolition.

His friend suggested they share the building drawing, and he would do a quick analysis and suggest the layout for the explosives.

Then not much later in the morning the returned data gave them the point in time and the location of the build that they felt was the one they were looking for.

Zoe commented that the building was in the downtown area of Seattle not too far away from the space needle.

Bram was surprised that the location was in Seattle on Roosevelt Rd. He commented that the enemy seemed to be close enough to Dallas that the whole affair might be connected.

Bram got the supercomputer to break into the future internet and find the computer with the county building records. The building they planned to bring down was a ten-story building. This was larger than Bram had anticipated. He hoped that it was not too large.

He looked at the clock and realized that the team had spent the morning but were now ready to get the building drawings into the hands of Castor's building demolition friend.

Castor and Diane connected with their building demolition friend and shared the building drawings. He looked over the building and commented that the building was what he called light construction and would easily be brought down. The support beams would need to have explosive charges put on each column and on each floor. Then the explosions would start at the bottom and in close synchronization, each floor above would be set off about three seconds apart. The building should fall down onto its footings and the only thing that might not come straight down would be the dust. It would follow the prevailing winds.

Bram and the team had been listening and when the call ended, he commented that they were on track to a late afternoon Fold to the future with their Forward Payment.

He suggested they all go to lunch and that afterward they prepare their C4 charges, while the basement of the target building got checked out. He commented that Marcus and Remi had come up with a scheme to check the basement out using the scout bubbles put into a formation taking up the same space as their team Fold transport.

During lunch, Pat, Amy, and Lacy were sitting together when the team entered. Pat commented that things must have been progressing well because the folks walking towards them were smiling and talking to each other with open enthusiasm.

Pat asked Bram if the future had been visited.

Bram shook his head and said that after lunch the team needed to prepare the gifts they were going to deliver to the future.

Amy asked if they could be of help.

Bram thought for a minute. He quickly calculated the fact that the team would need to prepare close to one hundred blocks of C4 to be placed on each column in the building.

He counted heads and realized that each person that was currently involved would have to safely prepare ten blocks of C4. He thought that would be a challenge.

He replied that they actually needed to recruit a couple more folks and suggested that Linda and Mallica join them as well.

He said that they would work in pairs and Castor and Dianne would supervise them.

Remi commented that they would be working in his Lab, and they could engage all the lab folks and Lori.

Bram nodded and said that would make it make it feasible to get the preparation work done quickly. Each pair would only need to prepare two or three blocks of C4.

Castor shook his head negatively and said he did not want to be in the same room with a bunch of amateurs handling C4. He suggested that they check with the General and ask him to have a group of experienced Marines prepare the C4. He figured it would be routine for the Marines and it would certainly keep Bram and everyone else safe.

Meanwhile, he said that he would take the team through a practice of the placing and wiring of the C4. He commented they would each need to practice several times and that they needed to do it fast enough so that they would not get caught in the building. He said that placing the C4 was going to be dangerous, and they needed to take their practice very seriously.

Bram smiled and said that he wanted to hug Castor but then the two of them would need to listen to a ditty accusing them of some unsavory behavior. He suggested they contact Matt to get the help in preparing the C4.

Castor opened his eyes wide and asked if Bram meant Marine Chief Master Sergeant Matt.

Bram smiled and said of course that was what he meant.

Bram looked over to Pat and Amy and said that he thanked them for their offer of help, but he felt much better having Castor engage seasoned Marines to work with the C4.

Amy nodded and said that she felt much better as well.

Bram asked Castor for the best place for them to practice applying the C4 explosives.

Castor suggested they use the beams in the hangar and practice taping on blocks of wood about the size of the explosives.

Zoe said that she liked the adjustment that had been made. She added that she was eager to deliver the forward payment but wanted to survive and savor their success.

After lunch, Bram had just passed his exercise of tapping the C4 to a beam when Marcus and Remi came in smiling and shaking their heads as they came back into the hangar.

Marcus said that they had sent a scout bubble into the basement that had returned with a broom handle sticking into the bubble. He and Remi had parked that bubble next to Bramlet One where it looked like a little brother. The big brother had a boulder sticking out of the side and the little brother had a broom handle sticking through as if it had been trying to get to the computer.

Marcus went on to say that the scout had served its purpose and located a space that looked like it was meant to hold a truck or store pallets. He and Remi had then sent in the scout bubbles in the shape of their large transport bubble and verified that there was plenty of room to spare. They had agreed to send in a scout bubble a few seconds before the team Folded in with the larger team transport bubble to make sure the space remained empty.

Bram thanked them and said that losing one scout bubble was worth making sure that they did not end up with any object sticking into their bodies.

Castor thanked them and then told them it was their turn to qualify to hang and wire the explosives.

It seemed to Bram that somewhere, someone was coordinating their actions because as they finished practicing, the Marines that had prepared the C4 carried in ten boxes. They opened one box and displayed the C4 with connecting wires neatly rolled up and attached to each block.

One of the Marines explained that the wires were long enough to connect to the next explosive block, and he picked up one wire roll and said that it was attached to the explosive closest to the stairwell that led down to the next lower level and long enough to get connected to the wire from that floor and the wire below was long enough to reach the next floor down.

This would go on until the last attached wire was taken down into the basement and connected to the battery power that would be activated to blow the building.

Two marines carried in another box and when they lifted the lid it had six lead acid batteries that were connected together to form the power supply, and two terminals where the wires running down into the basement would be attached.

They pointed to an enclosed relay that had a motor attached to it. They said that the motor was set up to turn when it received a command that would be sent to the control box from the Fold transport. The signal to activate the explosives required two buttons to be held down at the same time.

Bram nodded and thanked them for making the teams mission possible.

Castor led the way, and all the boxes were loaded into the transport bubble.

Bram asked Marcus when they had to Fold to be at their destination in the dark of night.

Marcus smiled and replied that it could happen any time Bram desired because they controlled when they would arrived in the future no matter what time they left from the present.

Bram nodded and said he was having a hard time getting use to manipulating time. He said he had grown up with it always flowing into the future and now he had become the object that could flow.

Remi said that it was hard for all of them to keep from being totally lost.

Bram asked that they do one more thing before the Pay Forward Fold. He wanted to identify the leader of the group who had attacked them and learn where he lived and some personal details about his family.

Marcus said that he had the name and address and could send some scout bubbles to get detailed information.

Bram suggested that they do it immediately so they could complete their mission before the end of the workday.

Marcus smiled again and said that he could make their Fold back a few minutes after they Folded forward, and when they returned they could go home early.

Bram smiled and said that they should wait until they learned how long they would be in the future. He pointed out that no matter what the clock would say their bodies would log in the real time.

Castor came over and said that everything was ready. He had taken the opportunity to put weapons on the Fold transport for everyone.

Bram thanked him and asked that he see if everyone could get a Kevlar jacket to wear.

He then asked Marcus to get his spy bubbles launched and find out about the leader's family. He commented that he wanted their message to have a very personal touch to it.

Marcus looked up the information about the leader of the organization that was housed in the building and learned that he lived in Laurelhurst which was a very high scale Seattle community.

Their person of interest had been married for twenty-seven years and had a daughter that had just graduated from the University of Washington. He also had a son that was a lineman on the college football team and another son that was still in high school.

Bram asked Marcus to get a picture of each of the kids at some highlight moment. He wanted one of the family at the daughter's graduation, one as their son was playing in a football game, one of the youngest son walking into his high school and a final picture of the family in their backyard.

Marcus nodded and said he would have the request filled in about forty-five minutes.

Bram asked Castor to organize the team and talk them through the timing and sequence of placing of the explosives several times. He said he wanted the practice to be in the hangar.

Castor assigned Zoe and Eric to the tenth floor. Bob and Thomas to the next floor down. Marcus and Remi to the eighth floor. He and Linda to the seventh floor.

He then said that after Zoe and Eric finished on the tenth floor, they would do the sixth Floor, Bob, and Thomas the fifth floor, Marcus, and Remi the fourth floor and he and Linda would do the third floor.

Then he and Linda would go to the top and check all the connections and come down and check each floor. While they were doing that, Zoe and Eric would do the second floor, Bob, and Thomas the first floor and Marcus and Remi would do the basement.

Bram asked if Castor had forgotten anyone.

Castor smiled and said that Bram would stay in the basement and set up the explosion control center and test it and make sure it was responding to the control computer. Then when Marcus and Remi were through with the basement and all the wires were together, Bram would hook them to the terminal. Bram had to make sure that the kill switch remained open, and the isolating piece of plastic remained between the contacts.

Bram's job then was to keep everyone away from the box.

Bram nodded and repeated what he was supposed to do.

Zoe commented that she was sure everyone else would be as far away from the box as possible and they would be eager to get in the bubble and get out.

Marcus walked over to the printer and when he came back to the table that they were all standing around, he spread out the pictures that Bram had asked for.

Bram looked at the family name and said that it was the name of one of the leaders that had attacked the compound a few months ago in their current time and who had been killed when Lacy unleashed her attack bubbles.

He called Lacy and asked her to verify the name.

Lacy commented that she was surprised and wondered if this future relative had staged the attack because of the family connection. She commented that it would make it the longest family feud in history.

Bram smiled and said that it was not a family feud, and it was certainly nothing like the Hatfields and McCoys feud. This was perhaps a family obsession and a weird desire to get even.

He wondered how this person would have learned about the Fold connection with the past.

He said that he would potentially use the family feud reference in his message to the future.

Castor asked if it was time.

Bram nodded and replied that they go for it.

<u>Chapter 6: Forward Payment</u>

Castor smiled and commented that Orlando claimed that Bram was more of a Marine than anyone thought. He then suggested that the team be called the BTR or the "Bram Time Raiders" who were "Swift, Timely and Deadly" and they should make sure that the enemy in the future knew that they should "Make Peace or Die."

He then loudly said Oorah, let's go do it.

Bram smiled as he realized that Castor had just uttered a series of Marine jargon. He let out a loud "Hurrah!" and led the way to the team's Fold craft

Zoe, Eric, Bob, and Thomas all let out a loud, "Hurrah" and followed.

After first verifying that their target coordinate was still clear by Folding an observation bubble there, they made the forward Fold.

The Fold delivered them to the empty spot in the basement of the building. They all let out their breath.

Marcus then quietly said, "no broom sticks on my side,"

Zoe asked everyone to remain in the bubble while her team swept the building to ensure that there were no people in it. She asked Bob and Thomas to go to the top and work their way down. She said that she would start at the entry of the building and that she was expecting that there would be at least two-night watchmen. She said that they would bring anyone they found into the basement.

Castor and Linda began unloading the C4 boxes and taking them to the elevators. He said as soon as Bob and Thomas cleared the tenth floor he and Linda would start delivering the C4 boxes to each of the floors. He said they would open the boxes and distribute the C4 to each position where they would be attached.

Donna suggested that all the C4 get attached in their position first and then the wires get connected.

They both then said, "Let's do it" and began to move the boxes to the elevator entrance.

There were two elevators.

Bob and Thomas got on one and pressed ten and went off to the top floor.

Zoe and Eric took the second elevator and got off on the first floor. She pressed the basement button so it would go back to where she knew Donna and Castor were ready to load the C4 boxes.

Zoe stealthily located the two-night watchmen that turned out to be where she expected. They were just around the corner from the elevators and were surprised when Zoe came casually around the corner. She had a smile on her face and politely said good evening and said she was in to inspect the quality of the monitoring system. She continued to walk behind the desk. Once she was in place she pulled out her weapon and asked the two not to touch anything and to step out and away from the desk area.

Eric quickly pulled their hands in front and crossed their wrists over each other, and zip tied them.

They then guided them to the stairs leading down to the basement.

They took them over to where Bram was getting the control box prepared.

Eric asked the nightwatchmen if anyone was in the building. The two claimed that the building was empty.

Zoe asked Bram whether she should shoot them now or later.

Bram replied that they should be hand cuffed to one of the support poles and he would talk with them as he did his part of preparing their forward payment. He suggested they get to the top floor and do their part.

He then turned to the two handcuffed watchmen and pointed to his own weapon and said that they should relax and at the appropriate time they would be released and would be able leave unharmed. He added, "try to escape and I shoot both of you."

He then focused on setting up the control box so he could test it and get it ready for the wires that would be brought to him.

He asked how long the two had worked as the nightwatchmen for the building and learned that one had been in his role for ten years. He said that he normally was there during the day but one of the normal night watchmen had called in sick and he had volunteered for the night shift.

Bram casually asked what they thought of the top brass and was surprised at the disenchanted responses and the negative opinions that the guards expressed.

The older guard commented that he had stayed on because the pay and benefits were very good, but the brass deserved a kick in the butt. He described them as arrogant towards and disrespectful of the working guy. He was not sure exactly what the company did, but it seemed like they milked the stock market but produced nothing.

Bram listened and felt better about his Pay Forward package.

He asked if the two would be able to find another job.

They both commented that the job market currently was not good. They said it would be tough to get another job in the current job market.

Bram asked if the dollar was still the currency being used.

The guards both said yes and that it was the strongest currency in the world.

Bram stopped and took out his wallet and put a hundred-dollar bill in each of their pockets. Before doing so he asked if they recognized the money. One of the guards commented that the bills were crisp but looked really old.

Bram nodded and then suggested they go to the bank and check if the bill was more valuable as a collector's item. They might be able to offer it to a numismatist because the bills were at least one-hundred years old. He suggested that they say they found the two bills on the shore at Gas Works Park to keep people from flocking around the remains of the building and in an attempt to find more money.

Both of the Guards nodded and said that that story was a good one and the park needed more people to visit it.

Bram finished setting up everything and then prepared the Fold craft for departure.

He reassured the guards that he liked them, and they would soon be released. Once out they should get well away from the building because a few minutes after they were set loose, the building would come crashing down.

If asked they should let their big boss know that the building had been demolished as a warning to him that he should not try to kill folks that had done them no harm and that any attempt to get even would prove to be fatal.

The older of the two guards asked Bram who he was. Bram replied that he was who the owners had tried and failed to kill and that they were receiving a warning not to mess with him. He said if they did not heed the warning they would be surprised by the next step since he took no prisoners and left all who opposed him dead.

As he finished his discussion, Marcus and Remi came down the steps into the basement pulling two wires.

They then went around the basement positioning the last of the C4.

A moment later, Zoe and Eric brought down a second set. They were followed by Bob and Thomas.

When Marcus and Remi brought their wires over, Bram checked to make sure the safety plastic was in place and the switch to the batteries was open.

He then carefully hooked all the wires up as he had been instructed to do.

Bram suggested that they take the two-night guards out and escort them well away from the building.

He asked the nightwatchmen if they had any problem just walking away and not looking back until they heard the explosion.

They both shook their heads and said they would do as they had been asked to do.

Zoe looked at Bram and said, "Boss you're getting soft in your old age. A few years ago, either you or I would have shot them between the eyes. Are you sure you want to let them go? They've seen our faces and can identify us."

Bram liked the drama that Zoe was adding.

He replied that he liked the two and they did not have to die just because they worked for people that were arrogant pricks.

As he finished talking Castor and Diane came to the basement and said that the building was ready.

Castor added just the right words. He asked whether he should shoot the two guards, so they did not have to have to be buried alive.

Zoe shook her head and commented that the boss had gone soft and was releasing the two.

She let the two loose and led them to the exit and took them across the street. She instructed them to walk away and not look back. She waited until they were a block away and then she and Eric double timed it back to the basement.

A soon as they were in the craft, Bram Folded out and once they were several thousand feet away, he sent the signal to blow the building.

At first, he thought they had failed, he put his hand on the plastic shield that had been on the contacts to make sure he had not forgotten to remove it.

Then the building seemed to be slowly deflating and starting in the basement each layer came to rest on the one below. It seemed that the building was deflating in slow motion. It was an amazing sight. What was even more impressive was the lack of any dust and debris.

The explosions were softly muffled sounds the created ten muffled explosions that seemed to signal the next level to slowly lower itself down.

When the last layer settled the pile of rubble was an almost perfect thirty-foot-high square.

Bram took the next step and Folded to the time at which they had originally arrived and to the coordinates of the leader's home.

The night was pitch black.

The coordinates put them in the open area in the family room.

The house was dark.

Marcus had been able to get the control settings for the light and motion sensors. They were able to quietly exit the transport bubble.

Bram put out the pictures that they had obtained of the family. He arranged the pictures in collage fashion on the kitchen table. He figured that once he imploded the building a call would soon bring the leader down into the kitchen where he would find the collage.

Bram wrote "don't mess with the past' on the refrigerator door with a large black marker.

Each of the pictures had a date on it and a note warning that it was personal, and any additional attacks would be answered in a fashion that would be very personal and devastating to the family.

Marcus said that he had placed the observation modules that were invisible to the eye but powerful enough to reach the very small relay bubble they would leave in the upper atmosphere. A more powerful and larger relay bubble was positioned on the surface of the moon and would constantly shift in time so that it would be almost impossible to find.

Bram checked the reception on his computer and said that it was time to Fold back to their time. They would be able to see the future from the Viewing room at their Fold work complex.

They Folded back at the end of their normal workday time.

Physically they were exhausted because they had been working nonstop for at least twenty hours.

Bram declared the next day was a work holiday for all of them and said they should all plan on sleeping in, but he would host brunch at ten.

He made sure that the feed from the future was available on his computer and then joined Pat for a ride home.

Pat gave him hug and asked how long he had been gone.

Bram shared that the team had been gone for more than a day but had decided to return on the same day that they had left so that no one in the present time would worry about them.

Pat shook her head and said that this new ability to do what she thought of as time travel was another complexity that the Fold capability had brought to their lives.

Bram nodded and said that the future for all of them was going to require a higher degree of disciplined thinking and a strong adherence to the principle of not trying to change the past to achieve the desired outcome in the future.

He added that inevitably there would be those that would try to alter the past and he had to come up with a way to prevent that from happening. He said that he planned to keep the ability of being able to go forward in time a secret. He shared that he had thought of changing the time frame of when to share all of the Fold capability out to one thousand years in the future but had been advised against it by Eric who asked, "what made him think that the aggressive culture on Earth that had for more than ten thousand years had been a continuous series of battles and wars, would change in the next one thousand years?"

Pat said that she agreed with Eric and pointed out the fact that sharing the capability at any time did not make a significant difference. If the bad guys in the future got that information they could travel in either direction and they would wreak havoc.

Bram thought about that for a minute and asked if Pat had any idea how to maintain the integrity of time.

Pat replied that Coke was an example of successfully keeping a secret to protect their brand. Bram had a brand called Fold. He had to keep the secret and pass it on to his successor.

She added that Bram needed to establish a Fold team that would be tasked with ensuring that the use of the Fold capability was used only for good. She suggested it be called the Fold Protection Team.

Bram replied that he had considered something along those lines, but the amount of Fold information seemed daunting. He then said that he would not release of the information into the future. He shared the fact that now that he had experienced traveling to the future to counter a threat because he had released the information, he agreed with her that they should revert to keeping it all close to a select team and keep it a secret. He commented that the teams name should carry some sort of powerful message.

Pat said that keeping it secret would probably be better. She also recommended that he choose the latest technology to store all the information on and put that information in a secret location and just pass on the secret location to members on the team.

IIc said that he would put the secret into a Fold bubble and the secret would be the coordinates of where the bubble was located and how the Fold bubble would go from coordinate to coordinate over time.

Bram asked her to remind him to set up that system the next day.

Once home and after a long hot shower, Bram fell asleep as soon as his head hit the pillow.

He woke up at nine the next day and when he got to the kitchen, Pat gave him a hug and kiss and a cup of coffee.

Bram sat at the table and slowly sipped on the coffee. He saw that Pat was getting the pancake batter ready and had bacon and sausage sizzling in the frying pan.

Zoe entered the kitchen and went straight for the coffee and joined Bram at the table. A few moments later Eric, Bob, and Thomas entered and sat down at the table with their coffee.

Pat asked what each of them wanted.

They all replied that they were after her famous pancakes with maple syrup.

She was placing the pancakes on the table when Castor and Donna arrived and joined them at the table.

Marcus entered and quietly sat down and said that he had left the kids down at the rec center where they were playing a game of snooker and being watched by Melisa.

Remi entered and sat down.

Pat poured Marcus and Remi a cup of coffee and put a plate of pancakes with some sausages in front of them.

The two of them thanked her and prepared their pancakes with butter slices before pouring the maple syrup over them

Bram turned on the large screen and connected the feed from the future.

Negative Fold

The kitchen in the future with the messages came into view. A few moments later, their nemesis entered as he talked on the phone. He stopped short when he saw the photos on the table. Each time he picked up a photo he would look around the room. He turned and saw the writing on the refrigerator and again looked around as if expecting to see someone.

He finally picked up the message and shook his head in the negative.

He tapped his phone, and a large screen in the family room came up that showed the collapsed building that the team had imploded. A newscaster was commenting that the two-night watchmen had reported that they had been escorted out of the building and then when they were a block away the building had come down as if it had decided to take a rest.

The newscaster asked about the people that had escorted them out. The older of the night watchmen commented that he thought they were associated with the mafia because the leaders underlings had asked about killing the two of them, but the leader had said not to do that. The younger night watchman commented that he was surprised that the leader was seen as the lead killer by the underlings because he had treated them well and with respect.

They both added that the team was very professional, efficient, and seemed to operate more like a group of Marines on a combat mission than mafia killers.

Castor let out a "Hurrah" that Donna repeated. He laughed and said that he was proud of the team giving the night watchmen the impression they were dealing with a Marine team. He was equally proud that Marines one hundred years in the future still had an impeccable reputation of being organized and proficient.

Zoe groaned and commented that she did not feel like a Marine at the moment but more like a tired old lady.

Bram quietly uttered "Yut" and complimented them for having brought the building down in a manner that looked like it was gently laying down to rest. He pointed out that very little dust had been generated.

Marcus commented that their Marine building demolition expert deserved much of the credit for their successful mission.

Bram agreed and asked Castor if his friend was married and had kids.

Castor replied that his friend was married to his high school sweetheart and had a boy that was eight and a girl that was seven.

Bram said that he would ask Linda to set up a scholarship fund for the two kids and that he was personally putting in an initial twenty-five thousand dollars into the fund. He looked around the table and suggested that they all owed Castor's friend big time.

Zoe said that she would put in ten thousand. Eric, Bob, and Thomas said they would match her.

Pat said that she would match Bram.

Castor shook his head and commented that his friend was going to be overwhelmed with their generosity and that he and Donna must be getting paid a lot less than they all were, but he was going to put in five thousand.

Dianne looked around the table and said that she would short her wedding dowry and match Castor.

Bram thanked them and said that he was going to recommend that all his bodyguards get some sort of reward from their employers but that he would personally pay the expenses for two, Fold weekend vacations for each of them.

Suddenly he stopped as a shiver went down his back.

He looked at Zoe and said he had a premonition and that he felt cold all over.

He dialed up Linda and quietly told her that he wanted her to smile, and then nod in the affirmative and hang up the phone, pick up her purse and walk out of the building and come over to the house. She was to act as natural as possible.

He hung up and asked Castor and Donna to double time and meet Linda but when they met her act as if it was a planned meeting and walk back with her to the house. If they were attacked, they should shoot first.

He looked at Zoe and asked her to sweep the house for bugs.

He asked Remi to get a Fold craft ready to Fold into the living room of their adversary in the future.

He asked Marcus to prepare to Fold someone into their new work center on Mataia.

He put up his hand when Marcus was about to say something and said, "I know." He then asked if Marcus if he could do it.

Marcus nodded and said he could do it.

Bram then said that the code word to make the Fold happen was written on the sticky note he had just given him. The sticky note was only to be read once the Fold to the future had occurred. He said that the coordinate for the person to be Folded would be three feet in front of where he stood.

Then he simply said "go" and everyone went into action.

Zoe returned and said that the house was clean.

A few moments later Remi returned to the dining room and said that the turkey was ready and should make a great lunch.

Then, Castor, Donna, and Linda came into the room.

Bram thanked everyone for their quick action and played back the scene in the future of their adversary in the kitchen. He asked them all to closely observe the person.

This time he kept observing the actions that occurred after the adversary had looked at the building going down. As they watched it was obvious that he dialed a number and said that the past had sent "them" a message and asked how "they" should respond. He argued that he did not think it would be a good idea. He listened some more and then said well if you insist, you're the boss.

Bram then went back and froze the scene the moment that the phone was pressed to dial a phone number.

He asked Marcus to record the number that was transmitted so they could trace it to its owner.

Marcus nodded and Folded a monitoring bubble into the future and captured the transmission. He then retrieved the bubble and sent the transmission to the supercomputer and a moment later he had the phone number and had located its owner in the future.

They were all surprised when they learned that the phone number was that of the director of NASA!

Bram shook his head in disbelief. He commented that it was hard to believe but it did make some weird sort of sense. If the future NASA director was learning the Fold secret, he might decide that eliminating those in the past that knew it, would then put him in control and he could use it to his advantage without worrying about it being in someone else's control.

He commented that they had found an evil Jeffrey as a Director of NASA.

He asked Marcus to determine the coordinates for the director and be prepared to Fold him to the same location that he had asked for the first Fold. The two Folds were to occur one after the other.

Marcus replied that he understood and would comply.

Bram led the way to the basement where their Fold craft was waiting. He got in and everyone took their places. The Fold put them exactly where they had been before. They then Folded their craft out of the living room.

They were in position as their adversary ended his call to the person he had referred to as "the Boss."

Bram Folded in, got out and walked quickly to within three feet of his adversary. He took in the look of surprise on the adversaries face and uttered the word "Payment."

Bram was just beginning to wonder if Marcus had acted when the adversary disappeared.

Bram walked to the kitchen, picked up all the pictures and the C4 but left the chocolate. He then erased the message on the refrigerator. He looked around to make sure that they had left no noticeable trace of their presence. He picked up the phone that his adversary had dropped and brought it back with him.

Castor simply said, "shoot first, ask questions later."

Bram got into the Fold craft.

A Fold later, Bram exited the Fold craft and led the way back to the dining area.

He asked Pat how long they had been gone.

Pat replied that if they had maintained the integrity of the forward flow of time they had been gone for fifteen minutes.

Bram checked the activity of the work area Fold barrier on Mataia and verified that two unauthorized entry attempts had been repelled.

They all sat in the Viewing Room and viewed the future, and they watched and listened as the wife of the target was asking the kids if they knew where their father happened to be.

Bram quietly said, "randomly everywhere."

He heard her say something about how nice he was to leave her the chocolate but wondered why he had left so early.

The scene made Bram wonder if the world would mature and how long it would take before a more gentle and tolerant society would create a world where treating others as one wished to be treated became the norm.

He looked around the room and thought about what each person would need to handle the emotional strain properly and effectively that he was sure they were all experiencing.

None of them had been trained or conditioned for the battles they had recently faced. In fact, as he thought back at all the attacks they had faced and come out unscathed he thought it was a miracle that he and they were still sane and functioning harmoniously.

He asked Linda to schedule some therapy sessions that would be both group and individually oriented with the Fold phycologist, Dr. Windal. He personally called Dr. Windal and asked her to work with Linda to set up some therapy sessions.

She responded by reminding him that he should call her Serena and that she would do so if he agreed to be one of her patients.

Bram knew that he had avoided sitting with her and discussing his emotions but this time he also knew he needed to talk about what had transpired and get it off his chest.

He knew that his decision of using the intrusion protection lasers to eliminate the two future adversaries had taken them all to their emotional limit. He was the one that had decided on that approach, and he felt responsible to find a way to reduce the strain on everyone.

He turned his mind back and focused on the next priority. His next actions needed to be a return to his past to prevent himself from sending out the time capsule with the information. It made him wonder about all the stories of the effect of a person meeting himself in the past. He would need to think through how to stop himself from taking an action that he already had taken.

Chapter 7: Future History

Bram sat in the viewing room waiting for the team members to gather and sit down. He was thinking through what his next step needed to be and how he might handle the situation.

He gazed at the phone from the future that he held in his hand. It was very similar to the ones that were currently available, but it was clear to him that as he examined it that it was a solid chunk of some sort of plastic. It clearly had a front and a back but both sides seemed to function the same. It was a trophy permanently associated with one of his more radical actions against the instigator of the attack from the future.

The three computers on table in front of him were taken from the attackers that had been killed when they attacked the team on Mataia. That was another incident that had left all of them psychologically marked.

Finding out more about that group was on the long list of to-do's. He hoped that there was not a follow up action required to prevent a similar attack.

Both events had a very negative connotation, and he wondered if the Fold program effort was worth enduring such attacks and then living with the forceful response to those attacks that he had so far been a part of. He corrected his thought and added, "that he was responsible for."

The information on the exteriors of the computer had provided the time marker in the future that had allowed them to find the time and the identity of those responsible for the attacks.

He and Marcus had not yet had the time to extracted the information in the memories of the computers. He was anxious to get into the computers and learn if there was any technical information that would be meaningful and useful.

He had put the extraction work to the back burner so that the immediate threat to them could be focused on.

He felt that the phone would allow him to identify potential future threats that might be associated with the two leaders who had been responsible, and he planned to follow up on them and their contacts next. But that could also wait until he had removed the Fold information that he had sent out to the future.

He knew that none of the attacks or the response of the Fold team would have been necessary had he not sent out the information to one hundred years into the future. It was a hard lesson to learn and to accept. It hurt.

Negative Fold

He knew that he had to move quickly to eliminate his own action of sending out the module with the Fold information. That meant an immediate trip to his past. He was uncertain how he should manage getting himself to not send out the information bubble.

How did one change the actions that had already been taken?

After thinking through several approaches, he decided to ask his team to help him out. He was sure that one of them would be able to come up with a way that he at the moment was not thinking of.

Once he had NOT sent out the information, he could be more confident that he had the time to set up a way to keep the Fold process details secret. He had come to the conclusion that he would need to slowly erase the Fold knowledge from the project records. He would needed to slowly dumb down the oversight committee and over time see if he could make the Fold project appear to be a failure.

He would need to study the hundred year out future in more detail to ensure that he had indeed removed all the Fold information from that time and then keep checking the close future to ensure that the Fold secret was being kept.

The far future, at least one thousand years out, needed to be examined to see if somewhere in time the competitive and combative nature of humans had decreased and a more peaceful society, which could handle the power that the Fold process unleashed, had emerged. He hoped to find a society engaged in the peaceful exploration of the universe.

As soon as he had that thought he thought of all the current combative situations currently in progress and he knew that he might find something similar even one-thousand years in the future.

The thought of space exploration made him think he should look in at the Swooshians and see how they had progressed over the same period of time. He was sure they would most likely have maintained their very inclusive and balanced society. They were the most stable beings that he knew.

He wondered if other species that might exist in the universe had been discovered in the future or communication from them had been intercepted. He knew that the Fold technology and a lot of luck had been responsible for them discovering the Swooshians.

He added the search for other intelligences to the Fold team's, "to do list." They would need to determine how to strategically execute such a search.

Once everyone was seated in the Viewing room he pointed at the trophies that they had accumulated from the future. He commented that they would examine each thoroughly but first he had to take the next step by himself and stop himself from sending the information to the future. He said that he was going to do this alone but was not sure of the best way to keep himself from sending out the bubble.

He shared he was not sure that meeting himself in the past would work. He said that maybe he had read too many science fiction stories that always highlighted a startling and shocking end to that occurrence.

Zoe suggested he destroy the bubble as soon as he deployed it.

Bram said that suggestion posed the same problem as telling himself not to send it, how would he know to destroy it?

Pat commented that maybe he did not need to meet with himself but needed some indirect way that would keep him from sending the information out.

She wondered if perhaps he would react to a message asking him not to send the information out.

Bram asked who could possibly get him to accept a message to not to send the Fold information out.

Pat took out a small perfume bottle and sprayed the mist on a red sticky pad. She wrote a message on it and handed it to him. She had written the current date on it and the words "Pat asks that you do not sent the Fold information to the future."

Bram read the message, he smelled the perfume and nodded. He smiled as he thought about the fact that Pat had saved him from himself several times. This approach was as imaginative as her use of a light flashing in morse code to give him a beacon home when he was lost in the negative Fold universe.

He heard her telling him to put the sticky note on the bubble just before his past self-arrived to put all the Fold information into the bubble.

Bram gave her a kiss on the cheek and said that she had just sent a shiver down his back and that he was going to see if she could reach back in time to correct his mistake. He commented that she had reached into the future to save him from one of his previous huge mistakes. He said that he was now going to trust her to keep him from making a huge mistake in the past.

He held up the sticky and said that he was going to work with Marcus and Remi to arrange his trip back.

The three of them went to the lab where Marcus figured out the coordinates of the desired spot in the lab during the time when Bram was to send out the Fold information bubble. Remi positioned the bubble at in current time in the spot it needed to be in the past time. Marcus then figured out the coordinates for both the bubble that would take Bram back and the viewing bubble that would allow all of them to see what transpired in the lab a few months ago.

He had to make sure the relay bubble that would send back the video would move about on the moon in millisecond folds so it would not be discovered.

Marcus did a quick run through with the observation system and then declared everything ready.

Bram noted that Marcus had become very proficient at determining the correct coordinates for almost any time and location that was requested of him. He planned to review what tools Marcus had created to facilitate such speed and accuracy.

They all went back to the Viewing room, and they all got a view of the past and the bubble that would send out the video to the future.

Bram got a hug from Pat, and she whispered to him that his past self would respond to her message.

He held up the red sticky for everyone to see and said "Hurrah" let "Pat save me from myself" and walked out of the viewing room. He and his small army of protectors proceeded to the lab with Remi.

Once there, Bram got into the bubble, waved, and made sure they were all in synch and then Folded into the Lab in the past. Remi had positioned the bubble in the current lab in the exact spot that it needed to be in the past lab.

Bram got out, walked around the table, and put the sticky note on the bubble that was sitting on the stainless-steel table where Remi in the future had been standing.

He saw a tape dispenser on the table and decided to tape the message to the bubble as a precaution to prevent it from falling off.

He walked back to the bubble and then Folded back to his own time. When he got out, he asked Remi how long he had been gone and learned that he had taken less than a minute. He and Remi and all his protectors walked back to the viewing room.

The chatter in the room ended as they walked in.

He walked in and sat at his chair. He commented that he was feeling a little weird and wondered whether he would actually respond to the message.

Pat reached over and held his hand.

The tiny monitoring camera bubble caught his arrival in the bubble. He stepped out and walked to the Fold information bubble and put the sticky note on it. As he turned he saw the tape dispenser on the table and took a piece and taped the sticky note to the bubble. The camera then showed him getting back into the bubble, Fold out and disappear just before his past self walked in.

His past self-put his computer on the table. He stopped after opening his computer when he looked up at the bubble and saw the red sticky note taped to it. He walked slowly around the table, and slowly reached for the sticky note. He carefully pulled it off and read it as he folded the scotch tape against the back of the sticky note.

As he read the message he was holding he looked up over his shoulder as if he expected to see a camera. The past Bram stopped and shook his head slowly and then read the note again. He brought the note up to his nose.

Bram now, sitting in the viewing, room knew that a tiny camera too small to be seen had indeed been where he, in the past, had looked. He then also remembered the smell of Pat's perfume in the past.

He watched as, he in the past, pointed his thumb in the air, kissed the note and carefully put the red sticky into his wallet. He, his past self, folded his computer shut and then stepped to the bubble and pulled out the computer that was in the bubble and then he Folded the empty bubble to its coordinates.

He shook his head and mouthed, "I love you too," in the past, and then waved his hand into the air as he walked out of the lab.

Everyone in the viewing room let out a cheer.

Pat smiled and gave him a kiss. Then said she was now waiting to be given the red or was it now a pink slip.

Bram commented that he was now wondering when he would be finding the slip in his wallet.

Pat said that it had been there since the time he had walked out of the lab.

He took the wallet out of his pocket and opened it. He shook his head as he pulled out a well-worn red sticky note that was now more pink than red and whose wear spoke of being in the wallet for a long period of time. He handed it to Pat and thanked her and said he was giving her the pink slip.

He looked around and asked if they all still remembered the Fold to the Future.

Zoe replied that the Fold to the Future was clear as a bell. She stopped, frowned, and pointed at him and in a quivering voice slowly asked who he was.

The room went silent. After a long moment, she laughed and said she was just kidding. She had just walked with him out to the lab and back.

Bram laughed shook his finger at her and then asked all of them to pay attention to anything that they seemed to have forgotten. He said that he had no idea how what he had just done might affect what they had done. He said that the pink slip in his wallet had not been there when he went to the lab and into the past to put it in place. He could not remember having it until a moment ago when he had opened his wallet and pulled it out.

Pat smiled and added of that if anyone had forgotten something, it would be a challenge to know what changed.

Bram then said that he wanted to check what had happened in the future.

He asked Marcus to capture the empty fold vessel when it materialized at the coordinate in the future.

Marcus nodded and after a moment commented that maybe that should have been the way they prevented the future from getting the information instead of having him use his intuition to accept the note from Pat.

Bram complemented Marcus on being a great Monday morning quarter back and that he agreed with him. He looked around and asked if he should go back and retrieve the red slip before his past persona arrived at the lab to find the sticky note and then return to the present to implement Marcus's suggestion.

Zoe pointed to Castro and told him he had permission to shoot anyone who agreed to that suggestion.

Bram put up his hands, commented he was not moving. He said that his experience had cemented the fact that they needed to protect the world from the technology that he had developed. He shook his head and said that he wished he had not opened up Pandora's Fold box.

Zoe commented that he should not blame Pandora. He had opened a different box that in the future should be called Bram's Fold Box. She added that his box was more dangerous than Pandora's box.

Bram asked Zoe, Eric, Bob, Thomas, and Remi to work with Marcus to check out the future to see if their Pay Forward actions had in any way changed.

He said that he was going to take trips about a thousand years up stream. He wanted to look but not interact with anyone. He was planning to look at the condition of the Earth, the Swooshian water world, and Mataia.

He asked Daryl and Harold the finders of the Water worlds, Mallica and Gerry the two that had facilitated the Swooshian Migration, Pat, Amy, and Erica, who had established Einstein city on Mataia if they were interested in making the Fold journeys with him.

Pat said that both she and Amy would absolutely love to see Mataia a thousand years in the future. She said that she personally wondered how much of their original work would still be in existence. She thought they had done a very good job of establishing Einstein City and they both had hoped it would last a thousand years.

Amy added that the trip would be a reward of her lifetime and that she hoped Einstein City would not look like Modern Rome with its historic ruins at its center. She wondered if after all the years whether any of them would be personally remembered.

Erica was all smiles. She thanked Bram for including her. She wondered if any of the original paintings that she had paid a pretty penny for had survive into the future.

Mallica agreed that seeing the condition of the water world would also be a dream come true for her. She wondered if the Swoshians had ever become under water structure builders. She wondered if they might have come up with the ability to create robots that could do work for them.

Gerry agreed with her and said that it was going to be a dream come true for him. He had so far been hard at work providing the Swooshians with the technology that would allow them to become builders of their world.

Daryl, and Harold the finders of the water worlds put their fists in the air and said that "their prayers had been answered."

Everyone agreed that their upcoming Fold journey was an extraordinary opportunity.

Bram added that it would be a reward for him as well. He commented that he wondered what of the Fold technology had traveled forward during that period. He said that at the minimum it would help to calibrate the actions that he was planning to take or should be taken and then learn the effect it would have in the future.

Bram said that after they took their journeys they would gather at his house and be served the meal of their choice. He wanted to spend quality time in discussing what they all had learned.

He asked Linda to take the meal orders and ask Chef D'Carluca if he could fulfill the order. He suggested that everyone in the viewing room plan to attend, and that Linda could decide who else should be there.

Linda recorded the orders and said that she would evaluate where to have the dinner based on how many people would attend. She said that her family would work with Chef D'Carluca and handle the setup and provide extra food if the gathering was large.

Bram asked if everyone was ready to begin their Fold journey to the future. There was a resounding shout of, "let's do it."

He then stood up and said they would Fold to the three destinations.

Bram asked those going with him to decide the order of the Folds that they wanted to make.

Pat suggested they visit the future Earth first to see how it fared and how society had evolved. This she thought would provide the basis on how to manage their current knowledge in their current time.

Amy suggested that they visit Mataia next to see how the world that they had established had progressed and grown. She thought it would be a good way for them to evaluate the work each of them were doing and would be doing in their lifetime.

Erica agreed with Amy and added that she hoped that Pat and Amy would be remembered.

Mallica and the Water world group agreed with the order. Then she said they were very interested on how the Swoshians had progressed, but they were just as interested in the first two visits.

Bram agreed with them that all three visits would be very enlightening. He reinforced Amy by stating that what they were about to learn would most likely affect what they would do for the rest of their lifetimes.

He said that he wanted to bring back a broad swath of information that they could study in their attempt to have the Fold capabilities contribute to the betterment of all the worlds over their lifetime and beyond.

Mallica commented that every day, every week, every month, the Fold technology was opening up a new world to all of them. Now their new ability to travel forward and backward in time would give them the ability to learn from both their past and their future. They could balance this knowledge to methodically prepare their race to grow and progress.

Amy commented that such knowledge could easily be misused or even when good intensions were at work, they could make big mistakes. They would need to become very disciplined and thorough in what they did.

Pat suggested that on their return they should all participate in a process to establish the guidelines of how to use the power that the Fold unleashed.

Bram said that he would get them together as soon as they returned.

He suggested that Zoe and those going with her verify the hundred year out impact that would happen when no Fold information went out. They should do additional Folds forward in time to verify that the Fold information had indeed been erased.

He said that the thousand-year Fold would start early the next morning at eight sharp.

Chapter 8: The Close Future

Zoe, Eric, Bob, Thomas, Remi, and Marcus went to the hangar and got into the Fold bubble. Marcus entered the Fold coordinates to take them to a point in time where the empty bubble that Bram had sent from the lab in the past should appear.

He had worked feverishly to determine when and where the bubble would appear. He wanted to retrieve it as soon as it appeared.

Zoe commented that they should be able to watch themselves arrive on their Pay Forward Fold. She commented that this ability seemed to counter everything she had ever heard about time travel to or from the future.

Remi added that it was something that he had not done much thinking about in the past so the whole topic made his head reel.

Marcus pointed to the screen where a small blip had appeared. He Folded over to it and had a robot arm grasp the small bubble and put it into the cargo bin. He then Folded to the far side of the solar system to be out of sight before Folding forward in time to check whether the Pay Forward Fold had occurred as they all remembered it.

Zoe commented that remaining undetected was tricky. She wondered if there were human outposts on the Moon, Mars and on some of the moons of Jupiter.

Eric said that there must be. They were one hundred years into the future. He expected there to be a significant human colony on Mars and a supporting launch terminal on the Moon.

Remi suggested that they fold observation bubbles to check out Eric's suppositions.

Marcus agreed and said they had enough bubbles to do so, and it fit into the scope of their Fold mission.

He spent a few moments working on his computer and said that he was deploying the observation bubbles to check out Mars, the Moon, Europa, and Enceladus the two moons of Jupiter thought to have the possibility of life below their thick layers of ice.

Marcus shared the fact that the planetary rotation of Mars was very close to that of the rotation time for Earth though its rotation around the sun was almost twice as long as the Earth's.

He let the team know that he had programed the observation bubble to skip in time around the circumference of Mars in one second Fold hops to get a picture that they could later study to see what had happened on Mars in one hundred years. He said that he was going to do the same observation on the Moon, on Earth, as well as the two moons of Jupiter.

He commented that they needed to come up with a routine to do the analysis and let their supercomputer do the initial scan and reduce the number of pictures to a manageable one.

Bob commented that he had been wondering what he might do once his bodyguard duties came to an end. He said that he had no desire for more of the same guard duty and there seemed to be little else that interested him at the Bureau. Thomas said that he too was looking for something that would capture his interest. He had thought to go into farming on Mataia with his father, but farming had never been an activity that drew him

Studying future history seemed intriguing. He had enjoyed studying Earth's past history and now he had the ability to study future history as it was made. He commented that he would request to be on the analysis team.

Marcus commented that he had found his calling. Bram had given him the job of a lifetime as the person that figured out the coordinates that a craft was to Fold to. That challenge had him constantly developing programs that would determine positions of objects that they were going to Fold.

The math, computer modeling and trips such as the one they were on provided a continuous, challenging and an interesting environment.

He said that Pat's and Amy's establishment of Einstein City and all of its associated elements had been a huge undertaking and had been a challenge that he enjoyed as well.

He laughed and said that Melisa's work in setting up the weekend Fold vacation spots had tested his ability to identify coordinates in buildings that were randomly scattered around the world.

He asked if anyone had thought about determining and maintaining the coordinates for a room that was rotating with the velocity based on its location on the surface of the earth. He said that every vacation Fold had to be recalculated before every Fold, based on the time and date of departure and again for the time and date of return. The whole vacation program if all the vacation spots were triggered at once would crash the supercomputer they had. He had created a safeguard program that spaced the Folds at a minimum one second intervals.

Zoe asked if they should be thinking about getting a second supercomputer.

Marcus replied that he and Bram agreed that they should not only have a second one but establish several on Mataia. Those super computers would focus primarily on the Negative Fold effort.

Zoe looked over to Eric and asked him if he had any interest in studying the history of the future.

Eric shook his head and said he would enjoy working with Marcus on figuring out how to place a Folded object in a very specific coordinate.

Marcus smiled and said that he could use the help.

Zoe commented that she had mixed feelings of what to focus on, but her future was not going be in the FBI. She commented that Bram was going to need protection for most of his lifetime and she was sure the Bureau would decide to stop the protection detail at any time. Her choice would depend on the politics of the day and whether protecting Bram was still a need.

Eric commented that protecting Bram would always be feasible as long as they could at the same time be doing other work.

Bob and Thomas agreed and added that such a mix would allow them to grow intellectually and broaden their skills while still keeping their bullet magnet functional and safe.

Zoe agreed that they could continue to provide the protection and grow intellectually.

Marcus said that his observation bubble was approaching the point in time that the Pay Forward Mission had arrived and that he would capture the entire sequence of what had transpired.

As they watched the building implode, Zoe commented that it seemed to be a job done by a group of professionals and not by a group of amateurs doing it for the first time.

Thomas pointed out that they had been following the directions of a leading building demolition expert and they were more like trained monkeys doing what they had been taught.

Zoe agreed but said it still was a rewarding sight to watch the building gently settle down.

Marcus pointed to two individuals dressed in what looked like police clothes that walked up to the corner of the street and stood there looking at the building and then turned away and left. He asked if they were the guards that had been escorted out of the building.

Eric replied that those were the two. He commented that they had speculated that the team was either a Marine squad or members of the mafia. He laughed and said that the comparison was a ying-yang one.

Marcus then Folded to the home of the person that had sent the attack group back to their time to kill Bram. He folded a tiny observation camera bubble into the family room where they watched the scene unfold. The initial placing of the family pictures and Bram writing the message on the refrigerator. It ended with Bram returning and signaling the Fold of the perpetrator and the NASA director to the coordinates inside the new facility on Mataia.

Marcus commented that he was still working with his therapist on the impact that it had on him when he Folded those individuals to the Lab coordinates knowing that they were going to be shredded into less than one eighth inch body pieces that would be randomly spread throughout the negative Fold realm.

He said he had not been prepared to be the person who, as in the movies showing the execution of the bad guy, pushed the switch to electrocute the person in the chair. He knew it was Bram's call, but it was his emotions.

He said that Bram was the judge, but he was not the guy pushing the switch.

Marcus shared the fact that Bram had put a block on the video so that the Fold of the two persons from the Future to the Lab could never be shown in slow motion. At Fold speed all that is visible is a brief flash. He commented that Bram had slowed the video of the bubble hitting the screen that he had shown everyone, by ten thousand times.

Zoe agreed that the emotions triggered by recent events had affected her as well and added that she too, besides attending the group therapy that they all were attending together, had several additional one on one sessions with the therapist to talk through the feelings that haunted her.

She added that her actions after the gun battle at the Mataia lab had been appropriate but counter to Bram's more loving motto of treat others as you wish to be treated. She shared that she had summarily executed several survivors from the future.

Regardless of how she felt, Bob said he supported her actions and that she had done the right thing.

Thomas pointed to the screen and asked if Marcus could focus in at what appeared to be a blinking light.

Marcus moved the tiny observation bubble to where the barely visible light was located in the ceiling, and they were able to make out that it was some sort of observation camera.

The only reason Thomas had been able to see it was that their bubble was located higher in the vaulted ceiling, and they were looking down at the observation camera from above.

Zoe asked if Marcus could determine where the signal went.

Marcus said that he thought there was a unit in the attic. He sent the observation bubble into the attic, and they were able to see the unit that was blinking as it transmitted the picture.

Zoe asked if they could figure out where the information was being sent.

Marcus interrogated the transmit unit and found the address it was sending the message to. He tried that address and after several iterations he said that it was going to a NASA location that was very near to the coordinates that he had used to pull the NASA director into the past into the laser barrier on Mataia.

He sent an observation bubble to the coordinates and discovered they were in a computer room. He was able to pinpoint which of the many computers in the room was the one that the signal was going to.

Zoe asked whether they could fold the entire computer back to their time.

Marcus said the computers were only as big as his countertop oven and he could Fold every computer located in the room back if she desired.

Zoe shook her head and said they should limit it to only the one associated with the person being observed. She then suggested they search the house for other observation cameras or listening devices and Fold those back to their time as well.

She pointed out that they would need to study who had accessed the computer to determine if there were any other individuals who had looked at the video.

Marcus suggested they move slowly forward one month at a time and see if there was any mention of their Pay Forward visit.

Marcus placed one very tiny camera/listening device at the home and then found what they determined was the NASA directors meeting room and put a unit there.

Their final monitoring was of the National News.

Then Marcus put them on a daily forward Fold journey for a month. That journey only lasted an hour in their time. They ended up with a tremendous amount of recorded audio and video that would need to be reviewed.

Marcus asked if everyone was ready to Fold back to their time and then asked how long should they have been gone.

Zoe suggested they return at the end of the workday on which they left.

Marcus nodded and said that they would arrive in the hangar at four-forty-five.

When they Folded into the hangar, Remi suggested they take their trophies from the future and place them in the large stainless-steel drawer of the now famous worktable. He suggested that they gather there in the morning and plan on how they were going to study what they had come back with.

Zoe said that she could immediately think of the categories of investigation.

She wrote them on the white board by the table.

Review

    1. Specific viewing content

    2. General computer content

    3. Computer software capabilities

    4. Computer hardware design

    5. Observations sensor design and capabilities.

Eric said that he was ready to go home and prepare dinner. He wondered when Bram and his group would be back.

No sooner had he uttered the words than Bram walked in.

Bram walked in as Eric finished his question and answered that his team was back and had a wealth of information that they would be spending the next few days processing.

Pat and the team had been right behind Bram, and she suggested that all go home and discuss their trips over dinner.

She introduced the person standing next to her as Marial and that they would all be able to meet her over dinner.

<u>Chapter 9: One Thousand Years</u>

Once everyone got into the Fold vessel, Bram initiated their first agreed Fold to one thousand year into Earth's future. They first Folded out very close to Neptune so they could determine where they could Fold to and not be seen. It became immediately clear that there was no place in the solar system where they could easily remain and not be found.

Bram immediately put them into a series of mini-Folds that lasted only a few seconds. This gave them enough time at each Fold coordinate to gather significant information about the condition of their Solar system and the condition on Earth. They were also able to intercept and capture the news feed at each Fold node.

Amy commented that Bram would have made a great combat helicopter pilot because he knew how to weave and dodge.

Pat said that one crazy helicopter pilot in the group was enough.

Amy counter that she was not a crazy pilot just an enthusiastic one and crazy was how enthusiastic pilots flew.

Mallica said the two of them had spent too much time together getting Einstein City built.

She looked at Bram and asked him if he was ready to take the two affected women to see what their handiwork had evolved to in a thousand years.

Bram nodded and said he had gathered enough Earth material that they would tie up one supercomputer trying to analyze it all.

He was ready to see what Mataia had transitioned to be.

Daryl commented that when he and Harold had found Mataia and Marcus had summarily put it into the not interested pile of other worlds they had found, they had been disappointed. He was now really interested in what had become of their planet. He was pleased that it had come out of the pile and had been selected as a second place where humans could migrate.

Harold added that he wondered how many people now existed on Earth and on Mataia.

Bram replied that he and Marcus had select Mataia and rescued it from the proverbial pile when he was looking for a way to protect humans from themselves. He planned to move his entire Fold operation to Mataia. At this point he was planning to first move the negative Fold work there.

Bram had no sooner Folded into Mataian space when he received a message asking him to identify himself. He was surprised but pleased that the Mataians were so much more awake than those on Earth had been.

Negative Fold

Bram responded with I and my companions are from your past. I am Bram Eric Nielson, the developer of both the positive and Negative Fold equations.

Silence from the challenging end was the response. Then there was the sound of cheering. The challenger came back on and said that they had arrived at the exact time that had been on record for a thousand years. They asked if Pat and Amy were really on the craft.

Then they said that the Terminal they had designed was still in use and it was ready to receive them and celebrate them as celebrities that were beloved by the almost one billion people on Mataia.

The speaker said they were in for a surprise.

Bram smiled and asked if everyone was willing to step into the future and learn too much about what they had done with their lives in the past.

Pat smiled and replied that she was personally very interested. She knew that it was dangerous to know too much about ones future but just as he had survived his ventures into the unknow Fold world she would survive and grow in a positive fashion, no matter what.

Amy said, "ditto."

Mallica said, 'let's do it."

Bram Folded to the Arrival Terminal coordinates.

The crowd in the terminal was cheering and a formal band was playing.

Bram got out first and was met by a person holding a microphone. Bram turned and as each person exited, he introduced them.

Pat and Amy got cheers and a resounding welcome that took a few moments to settle down. Then Mallica exited and the cheering was her name being repeated over and over. When Bram introduced Daryl and Harold as the two that had first found Mataia the cheers again went up.

Erica was the last to exit and for some reason the crowd went quiet. Then the cheers rose as they repeated, the art queen was real, the art queen was real."

Erica shook her head and quietly said that she must have done something that she was just learning about.

Bram chuckled and replied that she had just been told about her new career on Mataia.

He then introduced himself as the perpetrator that had caused the ripple in time that was still expanding across the Universe

The roar and the noise went through the ceiling.

He was greeted by a host of people that introduced themselves and were eager to get him to walk out of the terminal.

As he walked with them out toward the hangar that housed the work center, he saw the huge statue of himself standing with his left arm around Pat and his right arm pointing to the sky. Pat's left arm was pointing at Einstein City. Amy was standing in the arms of a person, and she was pointing at Einstein City as well.

Marcus, Mallica, Linda, Lacy, Daryl, Harold, and Gerry with his arm around Erica were around the base all pointing to Bram.

Bram asked if he could have a picture of the statue.

The person who had identified herself as the current leader of Mataia replied that they had prepared a complete history of Mataia and its development over time that would be part of the gifts that had been prepared in advance of his arrival. The fact that he had arrived exactly as predicted had righted what had become a question about the reality of what they thought they knew.

She asked that she be called Marial and said that her family name was also Nielson and smiled. She then let Bram know that she was a student of his and had spent many hours studying Mataian History and had also studied most of his work but understood very little about it.

She asked how he was preventing the future from going into the past.

Bram looked at her and said that her features favored Pat and that perhaps the curiosity gene that he possessed had traveled a thousand years into the future ahead of him and was now in her possession.

He smiled and thanked her for the question and truthfully replied that he had no clue because he had yet to do that, but he would send her the answer once he developed the block. He admitted to having the thought and would implement it to prevent people from trying to alter the past to satisfy some desire in the future.

She smiled and said that he would be very successful in the block that he had created. It had been in place and impregnable for the past one thousand years. She was aware of dozens of teams who had put their minds using the information on record to see if they could find the secret.

She turned to Pat and asked what it was like to live with a person who seemed to think universe changing thoughts.

Pat smiled and commented that it was a pleasant challenge and that she never competed with Bram in the technical realm but often had to rescue him in the social and political realm or to save him from himself and the risks he was willing to take in his endeavor to explore the Universes he had opened with a technology that was both a boon and a perhaps fatal one to all intelligent beings.

Their host smiled and said that Pat was helping put a sense of life and reality into a history that had over a thousand years grown into mythology. She admitted that though she had wished it were all true she had until the very moment of the call been ready for disappointment.

She asked how long they could stay.

Bram smiled and said they were capable of staying any length of time they desired but they were actually on their normal daily work cycle and were visiting the future to get calibrated on their desire to do the right thing in their time. He said that seeing Mataia doing well put the icing on the cake for him. Meeting her lit a thousand candles that warmed his heart.

He then asked about the contact that Mataia had with Earth.

Marial replied that they had chosen to keep that contact at arm's reach. They were constantly and secretly recruiting desirable people from Earth, but they had kept Mataia a secret. As far as she was aware, Earth did not know that Mataia existed.

Bram nodded. He shared the fact that he had kept Mataia a secret in his time because there had been multiple attacks on him from people in his own time and he had kept his work a secret and blocked the future because of an attempt on his life that had come from the future Earth.

Marial shook her head and said that such details had not come forward in history. She said that she felt better about Mataia not having made closer contact with Earth. She then pointed out that he had not given Mataia the secret of his work. She asked why that was the case.

Bram replied that at that time he had no way of knowing how well he had recruited those that ended up on Mataia and that he felt obliged to protect humanity from their base instinct of wanting to control others.

Marial nodded and said that she hoped that what he learned about the current Mataian Society would allow him to at least give them the ability to Fold in their current time.

She said that as the current leader she had continued to follow his teachings.

Amy smiled and said that she should continue to fly her plane as she was doing until someday in the future more people followed Bram's favorite saying of, "treat others as you wish to be treated."

The crowd let out a thundering cheer as Amy's words were heard.

Marial smiled and said that those words were the opening words of the Mataian Constitution.

Bram said that was the best thing that he had heard so far. He asked how the Mataian society was doing.

Marial said that it was a challenge to live by those words when disagreements arose, but those words were constantly being referred to and it always helped. The population on Mataia was a constant point of discussion because when they looked at the Earth with its twelve billion people.

The people on Mataia then asked if they were under populated. Many of them pointed out that Mataia was the same size as Earth. She was on the side that felt the Mataia did not need a huge population. She felt that it needed just enough of a population to be truly self-sufficient.

She pointed out that their diversity of wild animal species was well beyond what was now left in the wild on Earth which had almost no wild space left. Making Mataia the planet that harbored all species in a natural balance was her objective.

Mataia had become the place of survival for a series of animals that had gone extinct on Earth. She commented that the great majority of the Mataian population supported the view that very slow, controlled population growth was the right approach.

Bram complemented the Mataian society for its well thought out approach to keeping Mataia a paradise.

Marial commented that a celebration dinner had been prepared for them and asked them to follow her.

He said that he was looking forward to the Mataian dishes that had been prepared for their arrival and that after enjoying them he and his team were planning to leave.

Marial replied that she hoped to convince him otherwise, but they should now focus on the banquet that had been prepared.

She said there was one dish attributed to a Chef D'Carluca called Blue Swooshian Spaghetti de Mar that had always raised the question of what a Swooshian happened to be. She had looked through all the historic papers she could find, and it was never referenced.

Amy laughed and asked Bram if she could divulge that secret. He said no she could not, but Mallica and her team could.

Mallica smiled and said that it was an honor to be able to reveal a thousand-year-old secret.

She paused and the entire listening crowd went silent.

Mallica said that Bram had made contact with an intelligent Alien community that referred to themselves as Swooshians. She then explained that the Swooshians were intelligent beings on a water world. She made the point that Bram had created a team that had facilitated the migration of the Swooshians from the system where their star was dying, to a water world where they were now located.

The listening Mataian public remained silent.

Marial asked if that population followed Bram's rule or the first line of the Mataian current constitution.

Mallica said that humans had a lot to learn from the gentle Swoshians. These were beings of extremely high intelligence as well as being as big as a blue whale. When last she had contact with them they had the same reverence for Bram as was being displayed by the Mataians.

She commented that the Mataian constitution was first written in her time, and it started with the same words that still existed in the current Mataian constitution.

A cheer again went up from the crowd.

Bram said that his team was going the planet of Swoosh next and there was one empty seat on their Fold bubble and if Marial wanted to she could accompany them and while there investigate whether it was time to establish a link between Mataia and Swoosh.

He suggested such a relationship should be one that provided both societies a chance to grow.

He made the point that the Mataian constitution pointed to a social norm that would want all intelligent beings to positively influence each other.

He made the point that social power was the potential for social influence and Mataia would have a positive approach to positive influence and power.

He was certain that they would find a water world that would benefit from Mataian influence and that the Mataian society would benefit from the Swoshian influence.

He felt that it would lead to positive change in both societies. He offered up the fact that when two societies interacted with the simple opening saying of the Mataian constitution a breakthrough of friendship and knowledge growth would be the outcome.

A cheer went up from the crowd and they chanted, "treat others as you wish to be treated."

Marial replied that she was eager to go with him to the Swooshian water world.

Bram smiled and said they should eat first and then travel toward a fresh future.

The crowd around the lunch table that was on a raised platform were all loudly enthusiastic. There was a human chain of uniformed men and women that was keeping them away from the platform.

Bram asked if they were police.

Marial replied that they did not have police as she had learned about from her studies of Earth, but they had a large organization that was deployed for crowd control or for storm relief if it was required. They were not armed and relied on their ability to work together as a team when they were being used as they were at the moment to control a large crowd. They would also take immediate action if the crowd tried to move forward in mass.

Pat took Bram's hand and guided him slowly around the table so that each person at the table had a chance to shake his hand and say a few words. It turned out that she and Amy were as sought out as was Bram. She got the gist that the two were given much of the credit for having established the foundation of the Mataian society.

Marial pointed to the seat at the head of the table and the two seats to each side and said that Bram should take his seat at the head of the table, Pat should sit to his left and Amy should sit to his right. She said that her seat was next to Pat's who she hoped was her great, great, great, great, great, grandmother. She laughed and said that she had no clue how many generations had passed but the person she was sitting down next to looked young enough to be her sister.

The crowd let out a roar as she finished and chanted, "Sister, Sister, Sister," over and over.

Bram looked at Mallica and commented that he heard the influence of Orlando coming up from the chanting that the crowd practiced.

He smiled and said that perhaps he did see some grey in Pat's hair and got a little kick in the shin.

When the main dish, Blue Swoshian Spaghetti de Mar was brought to the table Bram stood and walked over and took a picture of the large serving bowl it was in.

The caterers put a helping on his plate, and he took another picture. He knew that Chef D'Carluca would be absolutely astounded when he found out that his recipe had survived for a thousand years.

He was also going to share this fact with the Swoshians when they Folded to Swoosh.

His first bite told him that the name had survived but the original actually prepare by the Chef of his day had a deeper flavor but what was being served was very good.

He was now eager to get to Swoosh and then back to his own time to share a gold nugget that he had not expected to find.

He used his time at the table to ask about the location of the various cities on Mataia. He asked about a desert island and what lived on that.

Marial replied that the island was a mystery that had puzzled the Mataians for centuries. It was the only place where mice existed and thrived.

She then said that the information he was asking about was in the information that was included in the records module she was providing. She commented that the module would have the history, the current technology, the current political situation and all the issues that provided a challenge to Mataian society all included.

As Bram finished his desert and put down his spoon, Marial stood and announced that she was going to spent the next few hours with Bram and visit a water world that presented an opportunity for Mataia to have a relationship with another intelligent species. She looked at Bram and asked if he had any parting words.

Bram stood and said he was extremely proud of the Mataians, and the Mataian Constitution was a treasure that warmed his heart. He pointed at his team and said that he would not speak directly for them, but he wanted to complement them for having contributed to the creation of a society like the one currently on Mataia.

Now that he was aware of the situation on Mataia, he would likely return in the near future to this time because the people were so friendly, and food was so marvelous.

He then said that his Fold craft awaited them and that he would bring Marial back with knowledge that would take the Mataians through a knowledge growth spurt that they should all enjoy.

The crowd roar kept up as Bram, Pat and Marial led the way back to the Arrival-Departure terminal.

Once everyone was seated he let them know that they were Folding.

In the blink of an eye, they were looking down at a blue green planet that was all water. Bram pointed at a large structure that was rising above the water.

He said that the Swooshians had figured out how to build a transmitter tower that allowed them to create a more powerful Fold system.

As Bram finished making his statement, a call came into their vessel asking for the Fold vessel to identify its self.

Bram asked Mallica to give the reply in Swooshian. He let everyone know that what they would hear what would be said in English by the translation AP that they had developed for this situation.

Mallica smiled and nodded. She put on her mouthpiece so she could mimic the Swooshian gurgle that accompanied Swooshian speech. She said that it was none other than Bram and his team making a visit from the past.

Bram was not surprised by the silence, but he added in Swooshian that he hoped all was well and that he had not interrupted anyone's meal. Bram knew that this was a traditional polite saying.

Finally, a Swooshian came on and replied that legend had it that one day, Bram would visit and that he had just turned legend into a reality that far exceeded the highest breach that any Swooshian could make.

He asked if the first speaker that spoke perfect Swooshian might be the very famous Mallica Evenston and whether by any chance was Gerald "Gerry" Sooner present. There was momentary pause, and the speaker continued and inquired whether Daryl Narda and Harold Redat were also on this particular visit.

Bram replied in his best Swooshian that the team that had facilitated the Swooshian migration was indeed with him, and they sent their greetings and hoped that the krill were numerous, and the water was the perfect temperature.

The Swooshian with whom they were conversing replied that he was the fifth Swoshian in a long line from that migration date and he was proud that the tales of "Bram the Great" had been passed on from one generation to each of the following generations.

He stated that the tales include everyone that he just asked about and that they also included others like Patricia Fleming that was with you many times, may she be well.

Pat smiled and replied in Swooshian that she was indeed well and sitting with her partner and she had brought a person that was a family member that was from the time they were now in. She then introduced Marial as the leader of Mataia a planet similar to Earth that was interested in establishing a working relationship with Swoosh.

She handed Marial a microphone and let her know that her words would be translated and sent down to Swoosh in Swooshian.

Marial sent down her greetings of "may all be well with all of your kind." We on Mataia live by the saying, "treat others as you wish to be treated." I am hoping that Mataia and Swoosh may become close and be able to link our two worlds in friendship and in a pleasant interchange of learning.

The Swooshian Leader replied that the words, "treat others as you wish to be treated" was a saying that Bram had used with his Swoshian ancestor, and it was still in use on Swoosh to this day.

Bram was not surprised when the Swoshian asked why Marial had waited so long to visit.

He spoke up and said that he back in his own time had blocked the future from accessing the Fold technology. He said that he had not wanted the Earth to become too powerful and misuse the Fold technology. He had also kept the existence of the Swoshians as secret to protect them.

He had asked Marial to visit, at this time, with him because he felt that it was time that a bridge should be built between Swoosh and Mataia.

The Swoshian replied that Swoosh would welcome an interaction with anyone that Bram approved of. They trusted his judgement.

Bram thanked the Swoshian for his compliment by saying that the krill that he had just swallowed was the best tasting in the Swoshian world.

The Swooshian thanked Mallica and Gerry for making sure they had the best tasting krill.

Bram then asked if the Swooshian was a descendant of Ohaan or Anon.

There was a loud gurgle and then the speaker replied that he was Ohaan the fifth.

Bram smiled and asked if he could breach as far out of the water as Ohaan the first. That in essence was asking if he was as smart and knew as much.

Ohaan replied that as hard as he tried he could not breach that high.

Bram said that he hoped to have many more visits with Ohaan, but his time was running short, but he had an interesting story to share.

He let Ohaan know that this was the first time that his team had made the leap so far into the future. The goal was to assess if the three societies with which they were familiar with had progressed and reached a time when they could interact peacefully with each other.

Negative Fold

He said that sadly Earth had not made the desired progress but Mataia, a planet that had been discovered at the same time that the current Swoosh planet had been discovered had made significant social progress and deserved to make contact with Swoosh.

He shared that back in his time the keeper of the Earth Krill had developed a dish he labeled Blue Swoshian Spaghetti de Mar. It was recognized as the most delicious batch of Krill that anyone could possibly raise.

On this current visit to Mataia, he had been welcomed and they had served him a batch of Krill called Blue Swoshian Spaghetti de Mar. The skillful way to raise such a batch had survived for five Swooshian generations.

Ohaan gurgled and said that any society that would keep such a skill alive for five generations was a society that Swoosh should engage and learn from.

Marial replied that any society that inspired a person to herd the Krill so skillfully was one that Mataia looked forward to learn from and to share the best tasting Krill with.

Ohaan replied that Marial was making him hungry, and he looked forward to having additional conversations. He asked if Mataia had Fold communication capabilities.

Marial replied that area of the sea was currently empty of Krill, but she would see if she could guide a batch in.

Ohaan said he understood and added that she was sitting with the best Krill guide that had ever lived and he wished her good swimming.

Bram wished Ohaan good swimming and said that it was time to get to the feeding field. He then hit the Fold button.

Chapter 10: Mataian Empowerment

*M*arial looked out of the Fold craft at the inside of the Arrival-Departure hall and thanked Bram for returning her home.

Bram smiled and said that she was not home but on Mataia at the very beginning of its development. He said that he had made the decision to let her visit the origin of the myth and to return to her time with the technology that would allow Mataia to interact with the Swoshians and to have the capability to make excursions around the Mataian and Swoshian solar systems. He said that he would keep a lock in place that would prevent Earth getting to Mataia.

He said that he would supply her with a working Fold message transmitter that would allow interaction with the Swoshians. He made the point that the Swoshians had developed the Fold message transmitter as a means to send out a beacon asking for help.

He and his team had intercepted the message and had back engineered the Fold message transmitter so that they could send a reply. He pointed out that the message transmitter that they developed was more powerful than the original Swoshian one because the Swoshians lacked the capacity to create the power needed.

He pointed out the Swoshians never developed the capability to build the Fold vessels because of their lack of capability to generate the power they needed.

One of the team members that she would meet, Marcus Smith who he would introduce to her later, led a team that found the water world needed by the Swooshians. He pointed to Daryl and Harold and said that they were the ones that had searched hundreds of systems to locate the water world and in doing so they also discovered Mataia.

The Fold team built the Fold transports that the Swooshians used to depart from their dying world to the one where they currently live.

Marial shook her head and said that being around him and his team had inspired her to return and urge Mataia to take a leap forward in both technology and in exploring the Universe. She was amazed at what she was learning. She said that most of what he was sharing had been lost over time. Some of it was thought to have been myth.

Negative Fold

Bram said that he would be pleased to help Mataia of her time flourish and become the Fold powerhouse that they could become. He had brought her back to the beginning of the Mataia journey as a first step in empowering Mataia of her time.

They were all walking toward the Negative Fold hangar when a Fold vessel materialized in front of them, and Zoe and the rest of the bodyguard team jumped out and surrounded them.

Zoe approached him and asked what was going down.

Marial had taken a step back to where Mallica was standing.

Bram smiled and said that he was running a test to see if his bodyguard team was paying attention and was ready to do their job.

Castor replied that Marines were always ready but being ready did not matter. What mattered, "was to win the battle when you got there."

Bram nodded and replied, "Hurrah."

Marial asked quietly if every outing ended in such excitement.

Zoe heard the remark and smiled. She replied that it only happened when Bram wanted to test his protection team. She stopped and realized she was speaking to someone other than Pat and stared. She then asked if she was Pat's one thousand years in the future granddaughter.

Marial said that the people around Bram amazed her.

She nodded and said that she was Marial Lyn Nielson of the Mataian year one thousand. She shared the fact that Bram had arrived at Mataia of her time on the day that the story of his legend had predicted. Long ago a message had been mysteriously received that from all investigation was determined to have come from an earlier Mataia. That message had become a myth that continued to grow and become more and more important to the people of Mataia.

She said that when Bram messaged Mataia of his arrival, he set off a celebration that she was sure would continue for many days to come. The fact that the other legendary Mataian figures accompanied him made the event even more exciting.

Zoe said that she was disappointed that she had missed being there, but she and her team had been busy cleaning up a rather dangerous situation in the future and had returned with rather good news that the future Earth no longer knew of the Fold technology.

Bram let her know that she would be able to make the next Fold trip to the future Mataia with him.

Zoe asked if it was Ok to share in front of Marial.

Bram nodded and said that the secrets that she might share would be about a thousand years old when Marial was back in her own time, and she would be free to share them as she pleased.

Zoe said that when Bram and his team folded to Mataia, she had Remi Folded the equipment they had brought back from Earth's future into the Lab here on Mataia.

Negative Fold

Bram explained to Marial that the attack from the future had come from Earth one hundred years ahead. He explained that he had Folded the information of the Fold technology into that time frame thinking that it was far enough out that the world would have matured. He said that it was one of his major mistakes. He and his team had acted against the future after a major attempt to have him killed. Then he had gone back in time and corrected his mistake. He commented that Pat had been the person who had guided him in correcting that mistake.

The trip to one thousand years into the future was his follow up to see if there was somewhere in the Future where the breakthrough that the Fold technology represented could be openly shared.

He looked at Marial and said that what he was doing was taking that first step with her and what he had to share was what Zoe had referred to as Pandora's box on steroids.

Marial replied that she was familiar with Pandora's box and wondered what the Fold technology could possibly have that would be worse.

Bram replied that it gave a power that allowed all of history and time to be manipulated and potentially changed. It could be used to do immeasurable good or unbelievable harm.

Bram pointed to the building on the other end of the hanger. Once he was close enough, he threw the stone he had carried in with him at the building.

There was a brief flicker as the stone reached the laser barrier.

Marial chuckled and said that in her time that barrier was part of the mythology of the facility, she commented that it must have stopped working hundreds of years earlier and though she searched for a way to prove or disprove that myth she could not find out how it might have been powered.

Bram shared the fact that the laser that she had just observed was powered by multiple Fold bubbles around Mataia. The bubbles were battery operated and had their batteries recharged by Mataia's sun. He said that the barrier had probably died when the bubble batteries powering the lasers died. He figured that with no maintenance the battery life was probably about one hundred years.

Marial said that she had spent many hours enjoying the view from the third floor of the building ahead of them. She complimented Pat and Amy on the amazing buildings and houses they had built. She asked how they had been able to make such beautiful structures on Mataia.

Pat commented that all of the original construction of Einstein City and the Hangar had been built on Earth and Folded into position.

Marial asked if she had heard it right and that all of the initial buildings in Einstein City had been built on Earth. Earth was many millions of miles away.

Bram nodded and replied that was one of the awesome capabilities that the Fold technology represented.

Negative Fold

Marial pointed out that the Fold capabilities that Mataia currently possessed was limited to Folds within the Mataian planet. The Fold Scientist were besides themselves because they could not figure out how to make it happen otherwise.

Bram nodded and said that the current Fold limitation was one that he was currently thinking of so that it would provide Mataia society a way to easily move about on the planet but keep it from being used beyond that.

Marial said that his approach had been successful at having kept the Fold secret a true secret and the Fold capability limited to travel on and around Mataia only.

She asked about the approach he had taken on Earth.

He pointed out that in his time Earth had eight billion bickering people and, in her time, it was up to twelve billion bickering people. He said that it was hard to imagine the economic and cultural upheaval that the Fold technology represented for the Earth at either time period. He had chosen to lock them out entirely.

He made the point that the change for Mataia in her time would still be a risk, but it would be a manageable one.

He then asked if she thought she wanted to try to incorporate the Fold technology. He said if she did not he could check out Mataia some five hundred years earlier.

Marial looked at Pat and asked if Bram was always so accommodating.

Pat replied that Bram worked at Bram speed and on Bram decision making and both were very fast.

Marial replied that she would guide Mataia through the change and do it in a fashion were everyone would benefit. She commented that Mataians would rise to the occasion and leverage this new capability to improve not only Mataia but to learn about the universe around them. She envisioned a Mataian race to the stars and to the far reaches of the Universe.

Bram nodded and said that was his belief and why he had decided to make the offer of slowly releasing the Fold capability to her time.

He asked Zoe to get Marcus and Remi to Fold to Mataia. He said he wanted to introduce the two to Marial and he was going to ask Remi to prepare one of the larger Fold vessels for Marial to take with her when she returned to the future Mataia.

He wanted Marcus to work with Pat to prepare a Fold Message Transmitter and the associated peripherals to be transported to Mataia so Marial would be able to communicate with the Swoshians.

Marial asked how long the preparation would take.

Bram replied that it would take about one Earth day, but it would not matter. She would return late in the afternoon of the day they had left the celebration.

Bram then suggested they all Fold to Earth and enjoy some of Chef D'Carluca's Swooshian Spaghetti de Mar. It would allow her to compare the taste of the dish as prepared by the legendary Chef and the one they had enjoyed in her time.

She could also take in how beautiful and scenic the Earth was and rest up before returning.

Marial shook her head and said she was beginning to understand the complexity of managing the Fold capability. She said that she was still thinking of time as being linear and not something that might be manipulated at will.

Bram nodded and said that she was seeing only the tip of the iceberg.

Marial said that she was not familiar with that saying or what an iceberg might be.

Pat asked if Marial was familiar with ice cubes.

Marial said that yes but only in a glass.

Pat asked how high out of the water an ice cube floated and how much of the ice cube was below the water.

Marial said that she understood that most of the ice was below the water, but she still was not sure what an iceberg was.

Pat replied that berg in ancient Earth meant mountain.

She then described areas where giant pieces of ice would break from mountain high accumulations of ice, fall into the ocean, and then float with only the very tip out of the water. These large chunks were referred to as icebergs. And only a small portion of the iceberg was above the water.

Marial smiled and said that she now understood the comment. She said that Mataia did not have icebergs.

Bram said it was time to get back into their Fold transport and they would all Fold to Earth. Once they got there he would arrange to have Chef D'Carluca prepare his Swoshian Spaghetti de Mar for their dinner.

He was sure the Chef would be thrilled to know how long into the future his creation had traveled, and he would especially appreciate the pictures of his creation in the future.

Once they were in the hangar on Earth, Bram called Linda and asked her to ask Chef D'Carluca to prepare his Swoshian special.

Pat asked when they had returned.

Bram smiled and said that they were back for lunch on the same day that they had left but their bodies knew that they had been gone for more than twelve hours. He said that after lunch they should all go home and get some rest.

Marial commented that she was totally disoriented and wondered how they were all handling such a confusing situation.

Bram replied that they were still learning how to manage their time and really had not mastered handling time at all. They were all as disoriented as she was.

Marial said that it seemed that every passing moment she gained a greater appreciation for the complexity of managing the Fold technology.

Pat led the way to the cafeteria and the group arranged the tables, so the bodyguards were seated around the periphery of the group.

Marial asked about the arrangement and Pat pointed out that the bodyguards were in place to prevent any attack on Bram.

Marial said it was still hard for her to accept such attacks.

Chef D'Carluca came out of the kitchen followed by a line of servers who proceeded to set the tables and to offer everyone the choice of starters.

Bram introduced Marial, their guest from one thousand years in the future. Marial stood up and asked if she could take a picture with him.

Chef D'Carluca beamed and replied that he was always rewarded when a beautiful woman chose to have a picture taken with him.

Bram explained that his name and his recipe for Blue Swoshian Spaghetti de Mar was still being prepared one thousand years in the future. He explained that it had been served in the future to the team as part of a welcome celebration and he had the pictures to prove it.

Chef D'Carluca ask if could sit down for a moment to look at the pictures. It was clear he had tears in his eyes. He asked the team how the meal had tasted.

Bram said that it was good, but he was sure that the one that would be served in the cafeteria for lunch would be better.

Chef D'Carluca looked at Marial and said that he wanted to hear her assessment once she tasted it coming from his kitchen. He looked at her and said that she seemed so familiar and then turned and went to the kitchen.

Marial sat down and said that there were no Chef's in her time because everything had been automated. She was going to have the picture of her standing next to the Chef put in the art museum in Einstein City. She said the picture of her with the Chef was a gem in an already very rewarding visit.

The Chef followed one of his helpers who was pushing a cart with a huge bowl that held his Blue Swoshian Spaghetti de Mar. He took an elegant plate that had a seashore scene as the boarder and was finished on the edge with a gold band. He said that the plate had been his great, great grandmothers and had not been used since he had come to the US. He made filling it a production. Once he had it arranged and garnished the way he wanted it, he placed in front of Marial.

He then signaled his helpers to serve the rest of those sitting at the tables.

Pat noted the fact the Chef had always focused on Bram but this time his focus was on Marial. He followed her every bite.

Marial had closed her eyes and was slowly eating the spaghetti and had forked in a clam. When she opened her eyes she stood up and gave Chef D'Carluca a hug and said that she had never eaten food that had taken her to heaven and beyond.

Pat took a bite and agreed that it was superb, and she noted how much better it was as compared to the one in the future.

She heard the Chef agreeing to send a serving with Marial when she returned to the future.

At the end of the meal Bram stood up and thanked Chef D'Carluca for one of the best meals he had ever eaten.

He then said it was time to go home and get some sleep. He stood up to lead the way out of the cafeteria. His protection team surrounded him and took the lead. Once out at the van convoy they got Bram and his team into the center van.

Marial chuckled and said that she wished she could take one of the vans and display it in the Antiquity Museum. She asked why it took so many people to take them home.

Bram explained that the lead vehicle was a Marine corps armored truck capable of taking out a tank or an attack helicopter.

The van they were in could take the direct hits of a rocket propelled grenade.

The truck that came behind was a duplicate of the one in front.

This was the way that he got home every day. The way in to work had the same configuration but he normally jogged in and there were attack bubbles that monitored the entire area around the compound. He finished by saying that he had been attacked at least three time at the compound.

Marial said she was surprised that there was such a concerted effort to try to kill him. She then said that she had never seen a tank, nor an armored truck, nor a rocket propelled grenade. These were only mentioned in a few documents, but little was known about such things.

Bram smiled and said that the times he was attacked outside of the compound was something like ten times higher than the attacks in the compound.

Marial shook her head and said that maybe he needed a bigger army.

They arrived at the house and the van drove into the basement.

Pat led the way up the stairs into the kitchen.

Marial stopped and looked around and said, "Oh my." She pointed at the microwave and said that it was the same model that was displayed in the Antiquity museum.

She went on to say microwaves were no longer used. They were replaced with molecular activators that heated anything that was put in a space similar in size to the microwave.

She pointed at the stove and commented that gas was not used because cooking had been mostly replaced with the Meal Generator that delivered the desired dinner heated to the ideal temperature. The meal whether meat or vegetable were all mineral based. No plants or animals were killed on Mataia of her time.

She said that the kitchen was no longer a place to prepare meals but a place to pick up the meal of your choice that was delivered by the Meal Generator.

Thomas smiled and said it was time for him to move to the future, but he wondered if he would miss the Steak with blue cheese on it.

Marial smiled and said that meal was one of her favorites and when he came for a visit she would make sure he got to try the totally synthetic version.

She then commented that the Blue Swoshian Spaghetti de Mar they had eaten on Mataia had been prepared by several Meal Generators. She went on to say that she was taking the serving of the one that she had just eaten so she could get the Meal Generator adjusted to match the flavor she had just experienced.

Bram suggested they all call it a day and get to sleep early and then go into work

Marial asked what they did to fall asleep.

Pat replied that she just lay down and closed her eyes.

Marial asked why they didn't use sleep inducers.

Zoe replied she had an idea what a sleep inducer was but if Marial had any problems falling asleep she should just count sheep. She asked Marial whether she had ever used a manual shower.

Marial said that maybe Zoe could give her a quick lesson on how to properly use the bathroom and the bedroom. She was sure that she needed help. She did not know what a shower was but figured that it had to do with cleaning one's body.

Zoe smiled and said that Marial would have to reciprocate when she visited the future.

<u>Chapter 11: A Walk-Through Fold History</u>

The next morning the team was sitting at the table and having a cup of coffee as they waited for Marial to come down. When she cleared the stairs, she shook her head and said that she had counted nine thousand sheep before falling asleep. She said she missed her sleep solution.

Zoe commented that such dependence on a drug was not good and that in this current time it was called being hooked.

Bram suggested that Marial let nature do its job. Then he said that it was time to jog into work.

She thanked Pat for the change of clothes and asked if she could take them back to the future with her.

Pat said they were hers to keep.

Marial smiled and said that once back in the future she would give them back to Pat's statue in the museum.

Pat handed Marial a pair of new running shoes that had a Velcro strap. She had noticed that Marial was wearing shoes that had no laces.

Marial commented that Velcro was still in use in her time.

The team purposely chose a slow jog.

Then Donna launched a Ditty, and the team began to sing.

Soft but willing. So soft but willing
Counted sheep but couldn't sleep.
Brand new shoes are on her feet.
Counted sheep but couldn't sleep
Brand new shoes, are on her feet
Feet, Feet, catch the beat
Running, Running, Running
Look at her, Just look at her. Look at her.
A future heart, and she is smart.
Brand new shoes, couldn't sleep,
Pay attention catch the beat.
Repeat!

As they jogged towards the work center the entire Marine guard contingent joined in.

Bram was pleased to hear Marial join in and chant the ditty and see the smile she had on her face.

He led the team directly to the cafeteria and ordered his breakfast then sat down at the table. Pat guided Marial through the breakfast line and then sat down next to Bram.

Marial asked what the chant was called and asked who had created it.

Castor and Donna raised their hands and said that it was called a ditty. They shared the fact that that Marines were always thinking one up and then jogging to its rhythm. They complemented her for having kept up and said that she had passed the test when she joined in repeating the chant.

Marial said that she planned to write a book about her experience, and she would add the ditty to it.

Bram asked if Marial was willing to get a thorough understanding of the history of the Fold break through.

Marial asked how she would get that breakthrough history.

Bram smiled and said that he would take her on a trip through time but in the comfort of the Fold Viewing Room. He would follow the timeline from when he was first recruited by NASA, through the breakthrough and bring her up to the current time. He looked around and asked that everyone participate. He assured her that she would personally understand the growth that each of them had experienced and the reason for the teams dedication to the technology.

He looked around and added that none of them including himself had ever taken this journey so they would all enjoy accompanying her.

He asked Marcus whether he could calculate the coordinates to specific locations in the past and use his miniature camera bubbles to capture those specific moments in time.

Marcus replied that he could do it, but he would not be able to do it in a smooth seamless manner because the position of the Earth would affect the exact coordinates that he would need to determine.

Bram replied that he would narrate and having a moment between historic locations would work very well.

Marial put her hand on her heart and said that she was experiencing a wonderful dream and wanted to make sure she was not still sleeping.

Pat said that the shoes on her feet were real.

Bram smiled and chanted,

"You have brand new shoes upon on your feet,

You'll get a story that can't be beat."

Donna and Castor repeated the chant three times.

Marial laughed and answered with a chant in reply.

"I have new shoes upon my feet,

Willing, Willing, Oh I'm so enthralled and willing,

To get the story that can't be beat."

Bram said that he was going to lead a tour that would enthrall the group, including himself.

Erica shook her head and said that she had been on the upcoming tour and had directly experienced a great deal of it. It had dramatically changed her life. She said she did not want to miss Bram's version of it.

Bram commented that all of their lives were dramatically changed. He smiled and said that he had changed from a person resenting being personally isolated to a person whose life had become so threatened that he had accepted the FBI and the Marine Corps providing him a small army to protect him. He commented he had traded the isolation in the desert to an isolation from society outside of the Fold community.

Castor agreed but said in the trade Bram had stepped up. He added that Bram had three hundred full time Marines on site and about another one hundred observer Marines that flew the protection bubbles. He said that Bram was now one of the most protected individuals in any world.

Bram suggested they move to the Viewing Room while he and Marcus worked on determining the coordinates.

He ask Pat, Amy, and Erica to work with Linda to invite the team members that were not with them at the moment. He said that those that were located remotely would be able to view the journey later on the video that he and Linda would prepare.

Marcus said that he would link into the supercomputer so he could manipulate the viewing bubbles. He asked Remi to give him control of at least three of the tiny camera bubbles.

The tiny Fold bubbles were sent back in time and went down along the street outside of Bram's apartment. The viewers watched as a young and extremely professional looking businesswoman exited a black Mercedes limousine. It was a younger version of Erica walking confidently into the building and up the stairs to the door of the apartment on the fifth floor.

Her knock on the apartment door was answered by Bram, whose appearance looked a little disheveled as if he had been running his hand through his hair.

The smile on Erica's face seemed to be painted on and not at all genuine.

Erica, sitting to the back of the Viewing room laughed and said that she looked like the wicket witch of the East with too much make up on.

The current Bram giving the flash back presentation commented that he had found her a little overwhelming, but she had given him a plane ticket and said that all expenses would be paid. He had been so happy to have the US government showing some interest in his rough theories about the ability to Fold time and space that he had put up with a person he felt was rather pushy.

Erica added that as she looked at her old self it was hard for her to recognize and remember the person of that time.

Bram commented that they had all grown significantly since that time. He said as he looked at how he interacted with Erica at that time, he was surprised that she had given him the airplane ticket to get him to the meeting where he met a team who he felt had little knowledge about his theory.

The next scene on the screen was Bram arriving in Washington. Two men in black suites and dark sunglasses guided him to a black van whisked him away to the Pentagon. They then led him to a meeting room where a group of people were gathered to listen to him describe his theory.

Once Bram was in the room and seated, Jeffery Mikelson introduced himself and then went around the table introducing the "team" that Bram was to join.

Those in the Viewing room listened as Elizabeth Miller introduced herself as a Moral Theorist. The younger Bram of the past stood up and walked to her, shook her hand and the two hugged.

He froze the video and shared with those in the Fold Viewing room that she was a person who he had admired and followed for many years. He said that she was one of the persons whose theories on fairness had inspired him and her presence had impressed him enough that she had made him decide to stay in what he took as a fake meeting.

He re-activated the video and they all watched as he shook hands with her, and she pulled him in for a hug. The little drone captured her whisper saying that, "the team is fake, and it has been set up for you, but the desire of the government for him to pursue his theories was real. Bram had smiled at her and nodded his head.

In the Viewing Room, Elizabeth let out a little groan and commented that the little Fold bubble had too good of a microphone.

Bram laughed and said that her whisper had caused him to hesitate to refuse a role on the team, but that hesitation was meaningless because Jeffery gave him an offer he could not refuse.

He commented that her presence had been what captured his interest on being on the "Team" and made him feel less like he had been shanghaied.

He added that the other people in the room were of top talent, but they didn't seem to know each other and seemed to only know what he had written at a superficial level.

Bram shared that Jeffery was very direct and made him a top salary offer. He was told that he was getting the best possible deal but the choice about joining was not an option.

Bram stopped the presentation and said that they should all take a short break as he organized the next part where he was out in the desert.

Erica commented that the offer that Bram received was forty percent higher than her salary at that time.

A few moments later when Bram saw that everyone was back in their seats and ready, he turned on the screen. The view he was presenting was from high above the desert and looked down past a very large boulder to the building at the center of a large fenced in compound that had razor wire at the top.

A shiny red helicopter glistened as it sat at the center of its landing pad.

The sun rays reflected off the black photovoltaic panels on the building roof that provided most of the power to the site. A ten-foot-wide cleared area outside of the fence went completely around the compound.

Bram guided the small viewing bubble around the area to show the fact that the desert was very dry but there was an abundance of plant and animal life.

He then took them all into the building and his living accommodations. As the apartment interior came into view. Bram commented that the spacious and well-appointed interior had immediately impressed him. He commented that the deck was large enough to practice his Tae Kwon Do and Aikido.

He had added the early morning hikes into the desert to his exercise routine.

That is where he met his mouse confident and counselor who he named Einstein.

Marial interrupted and asked if Einstein City was named after a mouse and not the famous scientist of that same name.

Pat replied that she had run a contest to determine both the name Mataia and the name of the first city. Einstein was Zoe's entry for the cities name.

Next Bram guided the viewing bubble in close to the large boulder and commented that it was the place where he had spent many a morning waiting for the sun to rise and then spent time sharing his thoughts with Einstein.

The screen went dark, and Bram commented that what they were seeing was what greeted him when he arrived at the boulder a few minutes before sunrise.

The folks in the View room could just make out someone arriving to the rock, climbing up, and sitting down.

The sun outlining mountains, out to the right of the boulder, seemed to be cutting the mountains away from the dark of the night sky. The battle of light against the black of night caused the desert to take on a mystical appearance.

Then everyone watching seemed to suck in their breath as the bright line of sunlight slowly unveiled the desert as if it were a bride getting her veil lifted and getting ready to kiss her new husband.

It seemed as if a line of light was slowly advancing toward the boulder and waking all that it touched. Then the line of light reached the boulder and like a mountain climber slowly making his way up the face of a cliff, the sun slowly traveled to the point where it began to illuminate Bram. And then as if by magic a little mouse popped out of a hole in the crack of the boulder and scurried up to sit next to him.

Everyone in the Viewing room heard Bram say, "Hello my good friend, I hope you had a good evening. Here are a few sugary crumbs so that you will be willing to listen to my current theories and questions that you need to help me on."

Then after a lengthy discussion on how he might link the various theories postulated by people much smarter than he, they watched Einstein go back into the hole in the boulder.

The screen then went into a super-fast forward like mode and the boulder scene and the walk out into the desert repeated itself multiple times.

Bram laughed as he watched the scene and commented that he had never seen the desert in such detail so fast and that the only thing he recognized was the red streak made by Amy flying her helicopter because that red streak was pretty much what his experience had been in riding with her.

Amy commented that she loved him too and that he had told her that the helicopter ride was the highlight of his day.

Bram smiled and replied that for the whole time in the desert he never started a workday feeling down because his heartbeat was always at its peak from the ride back with Amy.

The next scene showed he and Elizabeth, Marcus and Mallika walking down the hallway and entering the meeting room.

He stopped the video and explained that he had skipped a year of meetings and that the meeting they were going to witness was a key meeting where the Fold effort changed.

Bram restarted the meeting, and the camera zoomed in on Erica's face.

From her seat in the Viewing Room, she asked who the witch happened to be.

Bram gave a chuckle and replied that he had no clue and that he had heard a rumor that a house had fallen on that person.

Erica shook her head and said that the rumor was not true. She said that her world had been blown up during that meeting when she realized that Bram was not interested in having power or in her role and that instead he recommended that she get promoted to a much better role. It was a moment that had changed her life.

The scene continued and the Bram in the meeting indeed recommended Erica for a better role. He recommended that Elizabeth lead the technical and scientific team.

There was total silence in the Viewing Room.

Bram again zoomed in on Erica's face to show the look of surprise and he turned it to show Jeffrey's face who also had a look of surprise.

In the Viewing Room, Elizabeth commented that it had become clear to her during that meeting that Bram did not need support of any of his team in the technical realm that he was working in. He was quite independent and engaged the rest of the team in philosophical discussions but seldom in the science he was engaged in.

Erica spoke up and said that she at that time had been upset that Jeffrey had given Bram the best apartment. She privately thought that it should have been hers. The person she was at that time figured she deserved it. Instead, she had been assigned a one bedroom on the second floor. Jeffrey told had her that she would only be there part-time and did not need anything more.

She commented that Bram had told them both that unless they quit playing games he was going to let the rest of the world know where he was located, and they should come and pick him up.

She shared that both she and Jeffrey were amazed that Bram had figured out exactly where he was.

Bram commented to the folks in the Viewing Room that he thought that both Jeffrey and Erica had expected him to want a bigger project role.

What he had wanted was to have control of his own time and activities and he did not want to feel like a prisoner being held in captivity. He commented that he had used the location exposure threat to emphasize that he was changing how he was to be managed.

He added that things did change after that meeting.

He said that he had one more scene before leaving the desert. Two figures could barely be seen walking along what must have been a path but in the dark it was not visible.

The taller person climbed up and helped the more petite person get up on the rock. They both sat down and once again the line of sunlight came quickly across the desert and climbed the face of the boulder.

Einstein came up the rock, climbed into Bram's hand, and curled up and then got out. Bram could be seen breaking up a cookie crumb. The camera zoomed in on Amy's face that clearly showed surprise.

Two bubbles could be seen floating between them. Bram moved his hand under the bubble to show that it was floating and stationary in the air. Then he pulled the bubble a short ways away and let go and it returned to its original location. Amy did something similar and then could be heard asking how such thing was possible.

Bram at that time answered that he had no clue but if he figured it out he would let her know.

The Bram sitting on the boulder told Amy to enjoy her breakfast fruit that was in the bubble. He had encapsulated an apple, a bunches of grapes in each clear plastic bubble.

He told her that she was the first to witness the breakthrough he had been working on.

Amy let those in the Viewing Room know that it was at that moment that she knew she was looking at a true genius. But not just any genius, he was one that seemed to care about those around him and look out for them. He was a person who took the greatest breakthrough that could possibly be made as a moment to share with a lowly helicopter pilot. She added that it was Bram that got her a seat on the very next astronaut class.

She said that he had never gotten back to her with the answer as to what made the bubbles float. She ask if he had ever figured that out.

Bram said that he had not yet figured it out.

He stopped the presentation and said that it was close to lunch time, and they would all go to lunch together and then return to finish the tour.

He stood up said that he wanted to say a few words before lunch. He shared that getting Amy into the astronaut class had taken a little maneuvering, but it must have been ordained because Amy introduced him to Pat and Marial was evidence that the introduction had successfully led to a long line of family.

He was pleased that Marial had agreed to listen to her family history.

Marial said that she had a curiosity question. Was the boulder still in the desert?

Bram said as far as he knew it was still there.

All Marial did was to nod and thanked him for the answer.

Bram then gave a brief description of what would transpire in the afternoon and asked if he needed to make any adjustments.

Castor spoke up and said that he wanted to get a Bram's eye view of each of the firefights he had participated in. He wanted those in the Viewing Room to recognize the fact that Bram had not only discovered totally new universes but was a battle tested hero in his own right.

During lunch Marial was very animated as she discussed what she had learned about the Fold discovery and the fact that her current time had no clue about the power of the Fold. It was described in their history, but they had no experience with it and had misinterpreted it as just a part of the mythology associated with Mataian history.

She said that she knew that on her return much of the Mataian history would need rewriting.

After lunch and once back in the Viewing room, Bram went quickly through the meeting with the US President and the demonstration of the Fold during that meeting.

Marial commented that she had never held that formal of a meeting with so many armed guards and apparent pollical aids. She complemented Bram on an outstanding demonstration of the Fold capability. She was impressed with the fact that he had been able to use candy to convince the US President and also amazed that Folding such small objects had used so much energy.

Bram commented that at the beginning he did not yet understand the power required to move an object. At the next location he was taking them to he would demonstrate his cluelessness, and he would recruit two people to rescue him.

He then went to an overhead view of an isolated warehouse in the middle of a forest. He kept the fast forward going and they all watched as the large electrical substation blew up three times.

Negative Fold

The bubble entered the warehouse and showed several large blocks of steel. He explained that the explosions of the substations had been associated with the fact that he had tried to Fold the larger blocks. He shared that the power company refused to rebuild the substation after the third explosion. He knew that he needed to determine how much additional power he needed.

He pointed to Mallica and Marcus and gave them the credit for determining the power he would need for the largest block. He had no idea where he could possibly find the amount of power to achieve the Fold of the largest block.

He added that he was so engrossed in getting enough power and continuing his development that he left both Mallica and Marcus stuck behind out in the desert.

He pointed to Erica and gave her credit for searching the area and finding their current site at Dallas. The Fold project took over the entire supply of electricity generated by the Dallas water generators.

He said then made a mistake of having the steel blocks transported by truck versus trying to fold them to the new site. He said he would highlight why that was a mistake later in the presentation.

Bram then explained that he was going to fast forward the bubble views and they would watch the construction of Wheel One and Wheel Two.

Elizabeth spoke up and let Marial know that Wheel One had the name USS Hood and Wheel Two was the USS Rainer and that Pat was the pilot of Wheel One and Amy was the Pilot of Wheel two and she had been the Captain of one ship and Bram the Captain of the Hood.

Marial thanked her for the explanation and shared the fact that those details had been lost in a thousand years of history.

Amy commented that she and Pat had been overwhelmed at being given the opportunity to be pilots of such an advanced craft. They had wondered how Bram had been able to obtain such prize assignments for two raw recruits.

Zoe gave a small laugh and said that we have all learned that Bram's management style is act fast and ask for forgiveness if any objection arises otherwise maintain a rapid forward attack.

Bram nodded and commented that he always selected talented people that he could count on. He said that speed had its advantage but in a moment they would all witness the risk that speed sometimes carried.

The fast forward of the construction of the bubbles was fascinating to Bram. He appreciated the effort that Jose Estrada the construction manager put in to insure everything was constructed with safety and construction integrity in the forefront.

Bram paused the presentation for a moment and said that since Marial was present, he was going to Segway to the scene where he knew Pat was going to be his soul mate. The bubble then took a arial view of the Atlantic ocean and came down to the interior of a very nice restaurant.

The view then took the perspective that Bram would have as two very good-looking women entered.

One was the young Amy; her dark hair framed a calm and serene face. She looked very different in her dark black outfit with a low cleavage than the other times when he had seen her in military garb.

The second woman was Pat. He commented that she had immediately caught his attention as he took in her long curly red hair, freckles, and green eyes.

Bram had the bubble pan the room as all the people followed the two women to his table.

Bram commented that he felt an immediate attraction for Pat. He took note that she was as direct and confident in herself as was Amy. The two were a contrast in looks and in mannerisms but both were stunning in their appearance

They all listened as Amy describe her training routine. She shared that Pat had finished first in the class and she had finished third. He congratulated them on their achievement and said that it qualified each of them to command one of the two, Fold, modules.

Bram paused the presentation and said he was going forward to the very first Fold of the Wheels. He commented that Folds were because of a riot outside the construction hangar that threatened to expose the top-secret Fold program.

Bram then had the viewing bubble looking down at a huge crowd that was demonstrating along the fence line demanding to see what was being built in the large hanger. He said that several years later they would solve the mystery of how the crowd had learned about the Wheels. They would link the leak to a Fold IT specialist who was having an affair with the NASA assistant Director. She would be discovered only after Wheel One had been destroyed by a missile fired by a small attacking group while it was tied down in the Dallas hangar.

Marial spoke up and commented that she had never attended any presentation that feature so many heart stopping scenes.

Bram restarted the video and reoriented everyone again and said that they were now looking at the empty Dallas hanger. He then showed the large screens that had been put in place to be the Wheel Control Center at the Dallas site.

The two, Fold Wheels were shown on the left side of the screen where they were still located in the hangar near Seattle and the screen was blank on the right side that showed the empty Dallas hangar.

Bram's back was visible as he gave Pat the instruction to Fold. Then the view was of Bram's face as the lights blinked and there was a delay of the Wheel One appearing on the right. It was clear that the blood had drained from his face and then the lights blinked again and Wheel One appeared in the Dallas hangar.

The bubble was centered on his white face, as the loud cheering from the hangar made it difficult to hear him informing Elizabeth that there would be a delay of the Fold of Wheel two.

The view changed to Bram walking up to one of the older substation transformers that had overheated but had tripped offline and had saved itself from blowing up. He was heard telling the person with him to get as many blowers as he had available and cool all the older transformers.

Bram stopped the presentation and commented that they had witnessed one of the perils of moving too fast. He had almost lost Pat on that first Fold. They had witnessed a scene that went through his mind every time he was about to make a Fold decision. He added that it was a scene that often went through his mind when he and Pat sat comfortably on their two-person recliner.

He said a prayer every time.

Pat spoke up and said that everyone on the Wheel teams had talked about failure and dying and had been prepared not to make it but had agreed that they were willing to be the first and to take a risk of losing their lives.

Elizabeth added that all of the people on both Wheels had agreed that they would take the chance, "no matter what." She said that it was very personal for her. Bram had made her dream of going to space a reality for a woman old enough to be his grandmother and she would go into negative space anytime he asked her to.

Bram said that he was going to go through much of the rest of the history in fast forward. He said that he would focus on a few highlights of all the attacks that he and those around him had experienced.

He commented that the first scenes of Fishing on the Rushing River was to set the foundation for the series of attack experiences that were to follow.

It caught the scene on the veranda of Amy thanking him for all he had done for her and his wishing her the best in her new romance.

Amy interrupted and said that up until that moment she had been concerned about sharing her feelings for Jose because she was not sure how Bram would react. She pointed out that Bram seemed to know exactly how to make that concern evaporate.

Then the scene changed and seemed to frame Pat with her red hair, light green blouse, trim dark green shorts, knee-high socks, and black booted long legs.

Bram froze the scene and then smiled and commented that it was not the beautiful woman that stood out so obviously that had caught his eye and impressed him, but it was the chest to ground length of the largest fish he had ever seen that had caught his attention and the fact that someone as petite as Pat was able to hold it up off the ground.

He smiled and commented that it was the scene that always flashed through his mind when he saw Pat.

He then reactivated the camera, and they all watched him come down the steps to help Pat carry the fish to the side, kitchen door. There they could all overhear Mike greet them and help put the fish on a wood block table. He congratulated Pat on catching one of the largest fish he had recently seen coming from the Rushing River.

Bram said that was a great fishing trip and one that resolved the direction of several love affairs.

He then said that they were now entering into a series of different attacks and then the aftereffects.

The next scene was of Zoe and Eric jumping over the recreation perimeter fence in their skimpy swimsuits as they were firing their weapons. The camera turned and caught Bram delivering a killing blow to one of the attackers as all four of his bodyguards shot and killed the remaining shooters.

Bram guided the bubble to the Recreation center and zoomed in on the two people that had been shot. He commented that his mind had unconsciously pushed him to action because he had realized that Pat was the next person to be targeted but after the three shooters had been killed the situation caused him to lose track of what he was doing.

He had forgotten why he had attacked the shooter that he had killed.

The bubble then zoomed in on Pat sitting against the back of the recreation center shaking and crying.

Pat spoke up and Bram paused the bubble camera.

She commented that the realization that she was the next target had a huge negative mental effect. She had gone to counseling after that, and it was slowly helping but she was afraid that she was going to lose her role as the pilot of Wheel One. That worry only made it worse.

Bram added that at the time he was confident that she would recover but decided to ask her to go fishing at Rushing river where they had experienced such a great atmosphere the first time.

The next scene was of the area along the Rushing River and the Bed and Breakfast. Then the camera framed Pat in almost the same pose as they had seen her a few moments before. It framed her red hair, light green blouse, trim dark green shorts, knee-high socks and black booted long legs and she was holding a very large fish.

Bram commented that he had convinced her to go fishing in hopes that once again experiencing a quiet time would help her recover.

He then said he would take everyone through a fast version of what happened.

Pat asked that he take their first kiss in slow motion.

This caused everyone in the room to say, "very slow motion."

He took them through going to the cave to avoid the threat of potential attackers.

When time came to go to sleep, the scene showed Bram getting into the top bunk. He slowed the video.

Pat said that this was the first time she had seen what had made her heart, beat feverishly. She said this was a clip that she would put on an endless do loop.

The explosion of the door and being thrown from the bed triggered the fast forward action and the next scene was of Bram seemingly ignoring the risk and rushing out firing his long gun and shooting the attackers.

Elizabeth made the comment that fools rush in while the rest of us run the other way. She added that what Pat had experienced on that fishing trip had made her one of the strongest persons on the Fold team.

Pat spoke up and said that it had nothing to do with fishing but everything to do with her first kiss of the person she had been afraid to approach until the very moment of that attack.

Castor let out a 'Hurrah!" and everyone in the room replied.

Bram then let the following series of attacks all play out at high speed. The noise and scenes of attacks filled the viewing room for fifteen minutes.

Marial was the first to say something. She commented that it was a miracle that she existed. No one on Mataia's history had experienced or knew anything about what her ancestors had lived through. She gave Pat a hug and said that she felt that she was hugging the bravest person in the world.

Zoe spoke up and said that perhaps now Marial could appreciate why a small army was guarding Bram. She then added that the reason Bram had gone to the future was to see if there was any hope of sharing the information that would empower humanity with the ability to visit throughout the universe and throughout time.

Eric then added that learning about the Mataian society a thousand years into the future would make the decision to move permanently to Mataia much more desirable for everyone involved. They would know that they were giving Earth a chance to change but it would be up to them to create the society that embraced the saying, "treat others the way you wish to be treated."

Bram said that he was now going to share views of all the locations on Earth where Melisa had secured Fold vacation homes so that Marial could appreciate Earth's beauty and then on her return she could share this with all those in her time. It would connect them with Earth without taking a chance at exposing Mataia.

Negative Fold

He said that Mataian's that were cleared would be able to travel to Mataia's past to visit their own history and from this time take Earth vacations.

Ron Mueller

Chapter 12: Fold Invisibility

*CM*arial thanked Pat and Bram for their hospitality and told them it had been a wonderful visit and one that had personally warmed her heart but one that would also empower the people of Mataia to grow and to become the people that the two of them had always desired them to be. She suggested they go forward in Time and see if that were true and if not they should return to her time and correct the situation.

She thanked Bram for providing her with a large twelve-person transport vessel and the Fold Transmitter so Mataia could communicate with the Swooshians. She was sure that the video of all the scenic points on Earth would be a huge hit with the Mataians. It would help to lessen the desire of one small group to communicate with the Earth of her time. She was sure that his invite for the Mataians to visit their past and to then be able to visit the Earth of his time would go a long way in reducing the interest of the future Mataians wanting to make contact with the Earth of their time.

She commented that the new coverage of the multiple armed conflicts on Earth would most likely be even more effective at reducing that groups desire to make contact. She shared that Mataia had none of the weapons that were used on Earth.

Bram commented that he had provided three small bubbles programed to return to the current time and ask for any help if it should be needed.

She now knew a tremendous amount more about the history of Mataia and the fact that there was also fierce deadly opposition that he and his team had to overcome to protect the Fold capability. She now understood that Mataia had been established to ensure that the Fold capability would only be used for good.

He commented that he had much work to do to protect not only Mataia but to keep Earth from attaining the Fold technology. He was planning to simulate a fatal flaw of the Fold technology and slowly remove all information of Fold capability from Earth records.

Zoe spoke up and said that the conversation had just let her know that she wanted to take on removing the Fold information from the records on Earth. She smiled, thanked Marial for being a part of giving her what she knew would be a lifelong career.

Marial gave a chuckle and said that seeing Zoe jumping a fence in almost no clothing and firing a weapon at the same time would always be embedded in her mind. She said that she envied both her great body and the fierce protective aura that she had displayed in action.

She added that it comforted her to know Zoe would be erasing the Fold information from the Earth records. She added that she must have been successful because in her time Earth did not have that capability. She wished Zoe a long and enjoyable career.

After a round of hugs, Marial went to the twelve-person vessel and was just about to close the hatch when Chef D'Carluca came rushing to the Fold vessel with a container that he said was a batch of Blue Swoshian Spaghetti de Mar.

He received a hug from Marial who invited him to visit and teach those in the future to learn once again to cook.

Chef D'Carluca said that he would be honored to be given that opportunity.

Marial entered the Fold vehicle, the hatch closed and suddenly the hangar was empty.

The Chef shook his head and said that he needed to get out of his kitchen more often.

Bram thanked him for thinking of providing a very personal touch to Marial's departure. Bram suggested that he set up an online Chef class and get both current students and those in the far future to participate. Then when he was ready to test the capabilities of his students, they would discuss a Fold into the future for him.

Chef D'Carluca sauntered out of the hangar with a huge smile on his face.

Bram commented that the Chef's interaction had catalyzed some of the ideas floating around in his mind. He realized that he could do something similar with the future. He wondered what it would have been like if the actual human Einstein would have had such an opportunity. Then he shook his head and knew that it might have accelerated the destruction of the Earth. He personally would have to be very selective about his interactions with the future. The future Mataia provided an opportunity, but he would need to contain his enthusiasm.

He decided that his first responsibility was to put in the Fold blocks to prevent the future from visiting the past or from going very far into their future.

He and his team would continue to be Fold explorers, historians and developers knowing that sometime in the far future their knowledge would empower the Mataian people of that time.

Knowing that he and Pat had a descent in the far future made him realize that there was an immediate action that he desired to take.

He knew that one of the first things he wanted to do was to formally ask Pat for her hand. She had unasked given it to him, and he knew they would be together until the end of their time, but he felt that he would like to formally let those around him know that he and Pat were true soulmates.

He decided that he would ask her at the Sunday breakfast. He spent a moment inviting folks to the breakfast.

He then thought about holding the wedding at the Rushing River Lodge in what he hoped would be a less exciting wedding than Erica had experienced. He felt that he needed to make sure that there were offspring that would eventually lead to Marial being born.

He gave Pat a hug and said that it was time to go home and get ready for an exciting Sunday breakfast.

She asked what would make it an exciting breakfast. He pointed at Zoe and said that she was cooking, and that the Chef had given her a new recipe for the pancakes.

Pat laughed and said that she would have to stay in the kitchen and see how Zoe made mixing and cooking pancake dough exciting.

They all were leisurely walking back to their house when suddenly several missiles hit and exploded as they hit the laser shield that Bram had put up around their house.

In what seemed an instant the entire compound was on alert and Bram and Pat were pulled into the armored carrier and the entire group was surrounded by Marines armed with a variety of light and heavy armament.

Bram wondered from which time the missiles had come. He looked at Zoe and asked if the one-hundred-year future had been cleared.

Zoe replied that they had brought back a computer that was being used to monitor their original perpetrators home. They had not been able to find who might have had access to that computer. That computer was currently sitting in the same lab table that he had visited on his trip to the past.

Bram commented that once the immediate threat was over, they would need to figure out who in that time frame had access and if they had arranged the missile strike.

The armored truck was too large to drive into the basement entrance, so Bram and Pat were hustled into the basement under full guard and escorted into the saferoom.

Bob and Thomas joined them and shared that whatever just happened it felt like a huge earthquake and all the cupboards in the kitchen had opened and much of what was inside had fallen out. They saw all the Marines and asked Castor what was up.

Castor replied he had no clue other than that the house had been hit by at least four missiles and had survived, so they should thank Bram for having put up and activated his laser protective shield and they should be glad that it had worked as well as it had. He said that they had missed the most beautiful display of sparklers that he had ever witnessed.

Donna shook her head and added that from her position on her butt she thought the world was coming to an end.

Bram went into his office and then put in a quick call to the General and asked him to follow up with his monitoring group to see if they could back track where the missiles had originated.

The General replied that the monitoring team had tracked the incoming but had not been able to intercept the missiles. They were already zooming in toward the source that seemed to be in a remote part of the forest. He said that it was definitely some local group that had somehow been provided with some very sophisticated field missiles.

Bram then called Lacy and asked her to check if any of the people she was following had moved any large sums of money to a new location and if they had, what country was that money moved to. He let her know that he was looking for a sum of money large enough to pay for several field launched missiles with war heads on them. However, the money was probably transferred in a series of small sums in an attempt stay under the radar.

Lacy asked if the request was connected with the earthquake that had just occurred.

Bram let her know that the earthquake was due to four missiles hitting his house.

He let her know that she and Linda were invited to breakfast.

Pat handed him a cup of coffee and asked when he had put up the laser barrier.

He said that he had put it in almost at the same time as the one that he had put around the building in Mataia. The one at the house did not go underground and it was open around all the entrance areas and ended just about head level. He had meant to mention it, but the recent activities had distracted him.

He commented that he wanted to put the barriers up for all the buildings at the compound, but it would need someone to manage getting it into place and then to monitor it. He said that one of the drawbacks was that birds were vulnerable, and he had wanted to see if there was a way to modify the screen. He thought maybe he could make the shield less deadly for slow moving creatures like birds.

Pat said that she would make sure that everyone was aware of the shield.

Zoe said that she would work with the General and Lacy to establish a process to put the shield in place for all buildings. She said that she needed more to do than guard a guy who seemed to guard himself. She said that the shield had just saved two of her partners and they all owed him for having put the shield in place.

Bram thanked her and said he appreciated her stepping up.

Bob and Thomas said that they owed Bram and that he wouldn't have to wash dishes for the rest of the year.

Bram laughed and asked if one year of dish washing was all their lives were worth. He shook his head and said they did not need to do anything extra. They were willing to put themselves in harm's way for him and that meant more to him than their concern to repay him for what had been an almost unconscious action on his part.

Negative Fold

What he needed was to keep ahead of the people who were willing to go to such lengths to try to stop him. He said that they were trying to stop knowledge about the world around them and that there was no way for them to do so even if they succeeded in doing him in.

Bram spent the evening sitting on the two-person sofa with Pat at his side. They listened to some classical guitar by Andrés Segovia, and he went through his mind thinking how he would erase Fold information from the records so that it would become non-existent on Earth.

The one step he was sure about was that he would immediately move all Fold work to Mataia. The work at the compound would be some supportive work but the fundamentals and all computer records would be moved to Mataia.

He would need to outfit the Fold building on Mataia with additional super computers and the labs with additional equipment.

Then the hard part of selecting the key personnel who were willing to leave Earth for good would need to get underway.

Bram was up early for Sunday breakfast. He had been pleased to learn that Zuri, Orlando, and Elizabeth were all going to be attending breakfast. This meant that everyone who he had envisioned being present when he proposed to Pat would be there.

He had worked with Erica to obtain a top-quality Ruby in a gold setting, for the engagement ring. She had made the deal, and they had figured out how to use the Fold technology to whisk it from Rio de Janeiro to Dallas.

She had commented that he had made it possible to wait to the last moment and still come through with an engagement ring at the very last moment.

Zoe wasn't sure what was up, but she had been around Bram long enough that she knew that he was going to do something where he wanted everyone close to him present.

Bram had anxiously waited for everyone to finish breakfast. He then put on the love theme from the Godfather.

Everyone stopped and looked his way.

Once he had all of their attention, Bram got down on one knee and asked Pat if she would spend the rest of her life with him.

Pat smiled and said that she would spend every moment possible with him for the rest of her life.

A cheer went up from everyone present as he slipped a large ruby ring on her finger.

Pat held it up for everyone to see.

She said that Bram listened very well and that she had described this ring to him many times. She laughed and said maybe she should have described matching jewelry.

Erica smiled as she handed Pat a jewelry box and said that it was her gift to celebrate the proposal that she felt she was responsible for, since she was the person who had recruited Bram.

She opened it to show everyone a necklace with a dangling ruby and matching emerald earrings.

Orlando stood up and said that he had a composed a quick ditty for them all to chant.

Pat, more beautiful than a flower
Pat the woman with true power.
Has Bram down upon his knees.
Has a sparkler larger than most bumble bees.
What matters more,
She has Bram down on one knees.
Pat, more beautiful than a flower
Has Bram down upon his knees.
Knees, Bees, Flowers
Pat, Bram, knees, the birds, and bees.

Pat thanked Erica for the earrings and then she looked at Orlando and commented that he, as always, had added meaning to her day.

Pat sat down and then began to cry. She had thought of this day but had not been prepared for the way it was all taking place.

Bram thanked everyone for their good wishes and said that they would all be invited to a fishing trip at the Rushing River lodge.

That brought out a series of comments about having an explosively exciting wedding that would either take place in the river or in a cave.

Bram laughed and said that he did not plan to copy Erica and have a wedding in the river but planned to have a leisurely one in the Lodge.

Orlando suggested that he put a laser shield around the cave and have the wedding there.

<u>Chapter 13: The Listener</u>

The festive atmosphere of the Morning breakfast persisted throughout the day. Sunday afternoon the entire team gathered in the recreation center were they celebrated Bram's proposal to Pat. Everyone in the Fold community had long recognized Pat's intense love for Bram. Her intense, ingenious, and unrelenting pursuit to save him from the negative Fold realm had captured everyone's veneration. They came to think of Pat as the ultimate and intense problem solver. She had enrolled everyone around her and had gained the admiration of everyone.

They lauded Bram's public humble display and the fact that the ruby engagement ring was what Pat had said that she had always dreamt of.

Pat was surrounded by those admiring her ring, necklace, and earrings.

Bram called Mike at the Rushing River lodge and asked if he was willing to hold a wedding in his lodge.

Mike let out a whoopee, and complemented Bram on catching the prize fish and yes, he would be honored for the wedding to be at the lodge.

Mallica had overheard Bram and asked about the possibility of making it a double wedding.

Pat had just got away from the throng of well-wishers and overheard Mallica. She gave Mallica a hug and said that it would be great to have a double wedding.

Mallica smiled and said that she had planned to share her engagement at breakfast but had decided that she did not want to compete with Bram. She laughed and said she was too afraid to be sent back to the desert where he had imprisoned her for almost a year.

Bram smiled and said that since she had picked his favorite Marine, he would make an exception. He then gave her a hug and congratulated her.

Linda asked what was coming down and when she found out she asked whether three weddings would be too many.

Pat asked who in the world had Linda gotten on his knee.

Linda gave a laugh and said that he was a long-time friend, Rafael Evender, who had stood by her when she was having a hard time dealing with Zuri's wheelchair bound and ignored situation.

She said that they had all met him in the attack. She said that when Bram was walking out one of the peers shooting. Rafael was walking out on the other doing the same thing.

Linda went on to point out that Pat had backed up Bram and her mother had backed up Rafael because she was covering Zuri.

She said that her mother and father were not yet aware of Rafael's proposal. She commented that they loved him, so there would be no issues, but she just had not yet been able to have the right time to share it.

Pat asked if the following Sunday breakfast would be soon enough to make it public. They could get Chef D'Carluca to cater an afternoon banquet at the recreation center afterwards.

She asked if it was OK to also give Mallica a chance to make her engagement public at the same time.

Linda replied that it would not only be OK, but it would be great.

That evening as Pat sat next to Bram on their recliner, she said she sensed that during the afternoon he had gone from being very upbeat to seemingly concerned about something. She asked if it was about his proposal to her.

Bram pulled her to him and gave her a kiss and replied that she was his anchor, and he was making sure she would always be with him to keep him safe.

He shook his head and said that it was the fact that Zoe had returned from the future with a computer, which had been hooked to a tiny camera in the home of the person who had attacked him from the future, was what was bothering him.

Both Zoe and he had assumed that the assistant NASA leader was the one doing the monitoring. He and Zoe had discussed this during the afternoon and had concluded that it seemed unlikely. They had agreed that such an assumption about the future was most likely worse than the old saying about assumptions.

Zoe had been quietly sitting and listening. She held up several devices that she said she had found when they had come up from the recreation center. She made the point that they were new plants, and they were from the future. It confirmed the fact that there was at least one additional perpetrator and maybe more.

Bram commented that he had been successful in sending an empty information bubble and that those in the future were now working off what they had been able to lift from the original bubble that had made it through before. The team needed to make sure they erased all information that might have been copied to another computer and it would most likely be a major undertaking.

Eric commented that they needed to write an application that they could plant in the computer systems of the future that would slowly erase any information about the Fold. He wondered if Linh and Duong might be able to write and install such an App.

Bram said that he had no doubt that they could. He said he felt like calling them immediately. They had been at the rec center during the afternoon.

Zoe said that she had already dialed the number. She put the phone in speaker mode and they all listened as she explained to Linh that they had a major software problem and would like to discuss it with her immediately. She asked if she and Duong could come over.

Linh replied that they were walking over immediately.

Zoe hung up and said that they had done exactly what she had hoped by not asking what was up.

Zoe then made another call and got Remi on the phone and asked him to bring the equipment in the lab table's large drawer over to the house.

Remi simply said, "see you in a sec" and hung up.

Bram shook his head and said that he was putting Zoe in charge of cleansing future and present computer systems of references to Fold. Her goal would be to eliminate all references to Fold that existed on Earth at any time.

Linh and Duong arrived a few minutes later and after entering asked if it was safe to ask questions.

Pat led them into the office. She offered them a choice of any beverage they desired. She said that they were waiting for Remi before explaining the reason for asking them to come over.

Remi's sec was more like five minutes but they all knew that he had most likely rushed from his apartment and gone to the lab and then had turned around and lugged the future computer system and the listening, camera unit back.

A van entered the basement and Remi unloaded the equipment from the future. He commented that he had brought a power supply system so they could activate everything.

Bram thanked him and complemented him on his resourcefulness.

After Bram explained the problem, Remi, Linh, and Duong spent the next half-hour activating the computer and monitoring system. Once it was powered up Remi stepped back and told them it was all theirs.

Bram asked that they check the system to see if a third person might have accessed the computer.

It only took them a few moments to get into the code by tying in the supercomputer to scan the two units. They then verified that there indeed was a third person.

Bram recommended that they get a good night's sleep and then early the next morning they would journey back into the future to repay the person or persons for their attack.

He sent a text message to Marcus, Castor, Donna that said that he would see them early.

The General called and asked what they were doing to make the future mad enough to try to rocket the house a second time. He let them know that the bubble offense team had taken out four incoming drones and then taken out the launch site.

He commented that the future was improving their tactics, but they had not yet grasped the full capability of his offense team.

Bram replied that he appreciated the update, and the rising sun would bring a bright new day.

The General grunted and replied that the sun always rose, and he would see him bright and early at work.

The next morning on the jog into work two large explosions at the perimeter of the site was enough to stop the jogging and Bram and the team made the rest of their journey inside an armored vehicle.

The General and Matt met them as they entered the building and walked with them to the hangar. On the way he commented that the future must be very afraid of what might happen and must have activated everything they could muster to attack and try to kill Bram.

Bram commented that they had the right to be afraid. He and his team were going into that future and would personally put an end to the attacks.

The General asked if there was enough room to send a few extra Marines.

Bram commented that if the Marines didn't mind sitting on the floor he would appreciate having about a dozen of them. He stipulated that Castor and Diane should be in control of the Marines.

The General nodded and said that he would make sure that all his Marines had the latest weaponry. He commented that Bram should make sure that Castor and Diane knew exactly what was expected.

Bram looked over at Castor and Diane and asked if they had yet thought of a good ditty to describe the General's orders.

Pat spoke up and said that she had a ditty for the team.

Sitting on the Floor.

Armed, and ready for a war.

The Generals dozen plus eight more.

All to guard Bram's life once more.

The future has no clue about the hornets from the past.

That bring a burning deadly sting.

A Sting delivered by the best.

No more the future will attack.

The Generals dozen plus eight more.

Armed and ready to go to war.

Bram smiled and commented that Pat was beginning to rival Orlando in her ability to quickly gin up a ditty.

He then asked the General to assign the dozen so they could all make the Fold into the future.

He asked if Remi was alright to standby with Marcus.

He intended to repeat the elimination of the person or persons in the future in the same manner as before. He would stand three feet in front of the person to be Folded. This time the termination coordinates would be his house in the compound.

Marcus commented that he could handle it.

Remi responded that he intended to be there no matter what and the two of them could later bemoan the fact that they were the ones that pulled the final switch to the execution chamber.

Bram asked if he could activate the switch himself.

Linh said that she could quickly put a line in the Fold command that Bram would be able to activate.

Bram asked her to do it.

Marcus thanked Bram. He said that it was a relief.

Bram nodded. He said that it was hard, but he also knew that the cycle had to be broken to prevent the situation from getting worse. He was sure the future would have more deadly weapons than their current time and he had to prevent them from getting used.

He said that he needed Marcus to figure out the coordinate of the individual in the future and enter it into the computer and he would do the rest. He then suggested that Marcus and Remi monitor the screen around the house and verify the execution.

The General agreed and said that his men would be able to handle almost any situation if it came down to a firefight, but it would be much better if the situation could be managed the way Bram planned.

When the dozen Marines arrived, Bram asked everyone to get into the transport vessel so they could Fold into the future. He commented that the first Fold would be into the Computer room that held the monitoring computer. They would get there one day before Zoe and company arrived to remove the computer that was receiving the information from the monitoring cameras and audio from the home of their first attacker

The objective was for Linh and Duong to find out who had access to the computer.

The two had become familiar with the program since it was the same computer that Zoe would remove and bring back with her to Earth in the past. They were able to quickly learn that the person who also had the ability to access the computer was none other than the NASA director.

Bram shook his head. He looked at Zoe and asked who she thought the director would be sharing the information with.

Zoe said she had no clue. She looked at Linh and asked if there was a way for them to tap into the phone system and see who the Director might be calling.

Bram asked that before they searched out the human connection, Linh and Duong should install the application that would seek and erase any mention of the Fold information.

A few moments later Duong said that the app was like a trojan horse app that would slowly get into all computer systems that connected with each other.

Bram then asked that they see who the Director was sharing information with.

Linh commented that they were lucky to be on the inside of what seemed to be a very secure computer firewall. She commented that being inside allowed her to scan the entire personnel call record. She commented that the director seemed to have lately often been calling two numbers.

One was a person in Miami, and one was a person in Seattle. The calls to the person in Seattle corresponded within a day of an attack on the Dallas Fold compound in their time. It appeared that the call to the person in Miami happened a day before the calls to Seattle.

Bram asked if the person in Miami was the one with the money, and the person in Seattle the one who was reaching back into the past to buy the attacks on the compound.

Linh commented that would appear to be a good way to explain the relationship, but she had no way to confirm any money transactions.

Bram said that they would eliminate all three, but he wanted to see if they could determine who the person in Seattle was communicating with in their time.

Linh suggested they get into the computer being used in Seattle.

Bram asked if there was a way to tell how the Fold removal App was working.

Duong replied that it was sixty percent distributed across the computer systems and that in another hour all systems would have the App functioning.

Bram asked the date and times that the last call to Miami and to the Seattle area had been made.

Once he had those times, he said it was time to arrange to listen to each of the calls.

Linh quickly listed those times.

Bram said that they would plant listening devices in all three locations and then listen each time a call was made.

Bram noted that they had been gone for four hours and suggested they Fold back to their time and have lunch brought to the Viewing Room and from there they would monitor the calls and the messages while they ate lunch.

Amy, Pat, Linda, Marcus, Remi, and the General were all in the cafeteria getting ready for lunch when Bram entered and let them know that he would like to take lunch in the Viewing Room so they could listen in to the future as some calls were made in that time.

Bram had arranged to have three screens displaying the feed from the future. The NASA directors office was on the center screen. The screen showing the Miami office stood out about three feet on the right side of the NASA screen and the Seattle connection did the same on the left.

The first discussion was between the NASA director and the Miami connection. The discussion was how hard it was to eliminate their target in the past and that a powerful rocket attack on the home of their target would be the most likely to succeed.

Then a few moments later the Miami connection called the Seattle connection and said the money was deposited in the account and the countermeasure they had agreed on should be executed.

Bram commented they had just listened in to the arrangement for the first attack that they had already experience.

He then said that they were monitoring the Seattle connection to see how the attack had been carried out.

Linh and Duong were monitoring the phone and computer systems in the future, and they spotted a Fold signal leaving the Seattle area and being received in present Seattle at one of the largest missile manufactures in the area.

They said that they had the number of that person, and that person was the person who had the authority to release weapons to specific buyers.

Bram asked if Linh could check that persons financial standing.

A short time later, Linh said that she had been able to determine that this person was sending large sums of money to an offshore account in small amounts that ended up being a quite large sum when all the small sums were added together.

She wondered why this person was still working since he had accumulated at least one hundred million dollars in his offshore account.

Bram commented that it was greed and the fact that it seemed to be a safe activity. The person did not fire the rockets but simply made them available to the radicals that were ever so happy to launch what they thought would be an attack that they would be able to walk away from.

Duong informed them that the App to remove all information about the Fold was now in all computers in the future.

Bram said that the goal now was for all the hardware that had been involved in handling the information get removed from the Future.

Zoe said that she and a few Marines could get that job done in the afternoon and they could then concentrate on slowly cleansing the current time of all Fold information.

Bram nodded and said that they all would then carry on the development of the Fold technology in their facilities on Mataia.

Elimination of the people would not be necessary once they no longer had access to the fold technology.

Chapter 14: Mataia Establishment

The sun on Mataia was just coming over the horizon as Bram sat at his desk. He noted that it had a darker yellow cast and seemed to loom larger in the sky then the sun on Earth. The few clouds in the sky looked very much like those on Earth but seemed lighter and fluffier on this specific day. The gentle waves of the ocean ran along the beach as if they were chasing something down along the shoreline that they could not catch up to. It held Bram's attention as he thought about what his next moves on Earth needed to be.

The actions they had taken to erase the Fold knowledge in Earth's future must have been successful. The people who had perpetrated the attacks had been eliminated and the Earth one hundred years in the future no longer had any information about the Fold process.

The attacks on him and his team in their current time seemed to have ceased but he feared some sort of residual effects that might have already been agreed to but were currently dormant might be activated.

As far as the FBI was concerned, Zoe, Eric, Bob, and Thomas were still providing protection for him. The four in fact were but each now had an additional future role that they were developing.

Zoe and Eric were working together to slowly erase the Fold knowledge from Earth's current internet and computer systems. It was an effort that would take them quite a long time.

They had enrolled Linh and Duong to work with them. Together they had written programs that were imbedded into the internet to seek and erase information that dealt with the Fold process. The trick was that they had to not only handle the internet, but they were checking every computer when it logged into the internet for any reference to Fold. One quirk they ran into was that the word fold often appeared in sewing instructions, cooking classes and origami videos or instructions. They had programed in a content checker to shield their program from such references.

Thomas had decided to study future history to understand Earth's social and economic situation over time. Bram and he had come up with qualitative data guidelines to evaluate text, video, photographs, or audio recordings to evaluate Earth's progress toward becoming a more inclusive and peaceful society.

Thomas commented that he really was into the qualitative research that had him studying the future in-depth by using grounded theory or thematic analysis.

Negative Fold

He shared that by studying things in their natural settings he was stretching himself to interpret phenomena in terms that the social environment gave meaning to them. He commented that some of the social changes just a few years into the future was making him feel like an old man.

Bob had chosen to study Mataia's future in a similar fashion and then provide Bram with the information of how his current decisions were affecting the future. This was a service that Bram came to rely on so that he could adjust his thinking or modify his actions so that he delivered improvements.

Linda and Lacy had agreed to work together to study the ancient history of Earth and had agreed to staying at least twenty thousand years in the past. This was Bram's attempt at keeping them away from getting involved in what was and wasn't true about the more recent human history from the time of the Bible to the current moment.

Lacy had most of the current antagonists of the Fold program tied up in court and making sure that they had little time to focus on disrupting the Fold program. She said that her participation with Linda would not affect her ability to continue her Fold offense against their more aggressive distractors.

The opposing party won the Presidential Election and got control of the Senate. The oversight committee was disbanded as part of the reorganizing of the various committees.

Bram was pleased with the change and let the team know that it was time to accelerate making the Fold effort invisible.

Senator Olivia Newton contacted Bram and asked if there was a role she could play in the Fold organization. She shared that it seemed that the Fold organization was fading from the political scene, and no one had come forward for more money to continue its funding. She asked directly if Bram was working to make the information disappear from the record.

Bram inquired if the Senator was willing to leave her current residence and move to Dalles, Oregon. He let her know that if she joined the Fold effort she would be a good person to help set up a governmental based Fold organization. He wanted it kept simple and said that she would have great insight on the workings of the business of governing.

The Senator agreed that it was an opportune time for her since she had not run for re-election and was currently looking for a new career. Bram let her know that she had a great role to play that he would share with her if she could visit him in Dalles. Once she understood the role he hoped that she would be so excited that she would immediately accept.

Her response was that she had no doubt that she would be surprised and would most likely be very excited about going on a new adventure, but she insisted that he address her as Olivia and drop the Senator from their discussion. She verified that she could immediately fly out and they could discuss the opportunity in person.

Bram said that he was looking forward to meeting with her and asked her to contact Linda with her travel information.

Negative Fold

In a conversation between them, Jeffrey asked to be included when it came time to pull the plug and disappear. Bram asked why Jeffrey thought the Fold effort would disappear. Jeffrey commented that his IT staff had let him know that he needed to ask for a new set of Fold information because theirs had been somehow erased. He figured that Bram had begun to purge Fold information.

Bram assured Jeffrey that he and his family were all welcome to continue to be included in the Fold family.

Jeffrey thanked him and then said that when the oversight committee had been disbanded, Charles Ford, the science advisor, had requested to get more involved in the Fold effort.

Bram asked Jeffrey to describe how Charles could contribute to the Fold effort. He personally had a positive feeling about Charles, but he wanted to get another perspective.

The discussion with Jeffrey got him to engage Erica. He asked her to vet all the potential persons that might be asked to move to Mataia.

Erica reacted in a very positive way. She made the comment that she had found the very best person to discover the Fold process, and she would make sure that those going to Mataia were those people that like herself had become true believers in treating others as they wished to be treated.

Bram thanked her and asked her how married life was working out.

Erica smiled and said that she and Gerry were no different than he and Pat and they were looking forward to his wedding at the Rushing River. She hoped that the wedding would be a little less exciting than hers had been. She said that she and Gerry were still recovering from getting wed by a crazy practicing layman in the middle of a freezing river.

Bram laughed and said it was the only way he could think of getting her, Gerry, and everyone else out of the ice-cold river and into a warm place to recover. He said it was one of the coolest weddings he had presided over. He agreed that he was also hoping that his wedding would be less exciting and held in the warm interior of the Inn.

When Bram asked Marcus about the move to Mataia, the reply had been that he was looking forward to the move, but he wanted to make sure that the school system there was set up before making the move.

His comment cause Bram to think about two people that he wanted involved in such an effort. The two people were Elizabeth and Melisa.

He was certain that Elizabeth would organize a great education system.

He wanted Melisa to continue to organize the activities that had brought the Fold community together. He also wanted to continue to maintain the Fold vacation system on Earth that she had developed and to set up a similar one on Mataia that would allow for well managed vacations to be available on what he considered their new home planet.

Amy and Pat had followed through on preparing every building on Mataia and on Earth for the laser shield that Bram had developed.

Bram had continued the development of the laser shield to the point that he had created a laser shielded vehicle. This represented a major breakthrough because it meant that he was now able to shield the Fold transports and any Marine vehicle.

Pat, Linda, Mallica, and Lacy were all spending a great deal of time arranging the wedding event.

Bram stayed away from the specific details that they were getting into, but he had a few things of his own that he was going to arrange. He called Mike and Mary and asked if he could come up and discuss making the four weddings as safe as possible.

Mike commented that his new doors at the cave were doubled armored with half inch steel plates and ready for any attack by Bram's well-wishers.

Bram was planning in putting a safety shield around the Inn and perhaps at the entrance of the cave. He was also going to try out his mobile shield by shielding the three vans that were taking him to the Inn. This would provide a field test of his mobile laser shield.

He installed the laser shield on each of the vans and let Castor and Linda know about them and asked them to warn the rest of the Marines to wait on his all-clear signal before exiting their vans.

He left the following morning with his small army and went up to the Inn.

Mike and Mary met them in the parking lot. They commented that they had several current guests, but they had made all the arrangements for the upcoming weddings. They had been in contact with the neighboring Inn's and had coordinated with them. Mary smiled and shared that the fact that their Inn was drawing so much business to the area had their neighboring Inn's asking how much money they were spending on advertising the business.

Bram said that for as long as he was working on his projects in the Dallas area, they had his business as often as he could take the time off.

Mike added, "and be able to afford to pay for all the repairs the place went through at each of his stays." He commented that the steel plates on both sides of the cave door had cost close to a thousand dollars.

Bram nodded and said that protecting the cave and the Inn was what he had come up to discuss. He picked up three large stones. He then asked Castor to get everyone to stand away from the three vans.

Once they were clear Bram activated the laser shield.

He told Mike and Mary that he had just invented a way to provide protection to an object. He then threw one of the large stones at the first van. A small multicolored flash appeared as the stone reached the van. He threw the next two stones at each of the other vans. Each time there was a multicolored flash.

Mike commented that Bram had just shown him a protective screen like he had seen in the movies only this was the real thing. Mary commented that she liked the flash of color.

Bram then threw a small pebble at the first van, and it produced a small sparkle. He said that the screens were very effective, but they were also very dangerous. Ones like that on the vans were dangerous to any one unknowingly reaching for the door handle.

Bram paused to shut down the screens and called out that the screens were deactivated.

Bram then said that he wanted to put the screen around the Inn and activate it during the weddings.

After the weddings, he would elevate the screen so it was held above the first floor and could be dropped into place if there was a serious attack.

Mike and Mary both commented that after the last wedding excitement they would welcome the protective screen. Mike added that he did not think the cave needed it. He was getting use to building ever stronger doors.

Bram said that he would make sure that the Inn's protective laser screen had very visible markings to keep everyone away from it.

Mike asked if Bram was expecting an attack.

Bram replied that he had been attacked several times since the wedding in the river and that this time he was trying to stay ahead of his attackers.

Mike laughed and said that the last wedding indeed had a chilling touch to it in more ways than one. He was OK with the plan to provide the Laser shield, but he wanted to make sure that there was no way that a guest could accidently walk into the shield from either side. He suggested that Bram erect two chain link fences about two feet apart that would go all the way around the periphery of the lodge and that the shield be between the fences. In that way the shield could stay in place for the entire time that the wedding and reception was going on. Afterward, the shield could be turned off and the fence removed.

Bram thanked him for suggesting the fence and said that he would send a crew out to put it up and asked that Mike let them know where he wanted the two fences.

Once they got back underway on the return trip to the Fold site, Donna and Castor began to chant a ditty they had come up with. They had their radio connection with the other two vans and instantly everyone was singing the ditty.

> *Got to see a laser show.*
> *Bram threw rocks and made them glow.*
> *We didn't know it could be so.*
> *Sparklers, Sparklers, what a show.*
> *Those coming at us just don't know.*
> *It is, it is, it is so.*
> *Shoot, shoot, shoot at us and see the show.*
> *Shoot at us and get to know.*
> *That laser screens are on the go.*
> *If we shoot back, there is a sting.*
> *The deadly part of a laser show.*

Bram chuckled and said that he was surrounded by raggers that loved to chant.

Bram enjoyed the camaraderie of everyone in the three vans.

They were driving along the two-lane highway on their way back to the compound, when a semi coming from the opposite direction moved from its lane in a maneuver intended sideswipe them and push the vans down into the steep almost cliff like ravine at the side of the highway.

There was a continuous brilliant streaking flash as the side of the truck making the side swipe attempt was vaporized. The three vans only experienced a slight sideward pressure as if they were being hit by a strong wind.

The truck lost almost two feet of its tractor and trailer. It slid down the highway on its side for more than one hundred feet and looked like a relic out of the junk yard. It came to a stop with the vaporized side down on the surface of the highway.

Bram quickly turned off the protection shield and yelled that it was safe to get out.

The Marines ran out and surrounded the truck and then pulled the driver from the cab. The driver had lost most of his left arm. It was not bleeding but cleanly cauterized and looked like it had been removed by an skilled surgeon. It was clear that the driver was in a great deal of pain and one of the Marines administered some pain killer. They put the driver in the back of the third van and covered him with a blanket.

Castor asked that three Marines stay at the accident scene until a Marine back up unit could be sent out to retrieve the Semi. He said that they were going to continue back to the compound.

He left orders that the semi was to be kept in the possession of the Marine corps.

When they got back into the van, Castor put in a call to have a team come out and get the semi back to the compound. He made the point that the semi was the property of the Marine corps.

Bram reactivated the laser protective screens of the three vans and then listened to Donna once again lead the ditty.

The attack had provided the best field test of his portable protective screen that he could have thought off. It had prevented a death ride for all of them down the steep mountain side ravine.

Castor reaffirmed his thoughts when he said that the screen had worked so well that the impact of the semi felt more like being hit by a stiff gust of wind from the side. He said that he was still seeing sparklers that the screen made from the two feet of the semi that it had vaporized. He said that it was an unbelievable experience and one that would be with him for a long time to come.

Bram nodded and said that before the truck had tried to side swipe them, he had no idea exactly how the protective screen would act but it essentially absorbed the energy generated by the impact and turned it into a continuous stream of material being randomly scattered in the negative Fold environment.

He complemented Castor on making sure that the semi got brought back to the compound. He asked that the semi be put in the hangar vaporized side up so that it would be easier to examine.

General Tilman was standing in the hangar when the three vans drove in. He saluted the Marines getting out of the van's and congratulated them on a job well done.

Several Marine EMT's took the driver of the semi and said that they were taking him to the hospital where he would be kept under guard. They commented that they had never seen a severed arm in quiet the condition as the drivers left arm. It was the cleanest amputation that they had ever witnessed

The General requested a demonstration of the new protective screen capability that Bram had developed for vehicles.

Bram nodded and commented that his newly developed mobile protective shield had gotten tested before he had been ready, but the result was all that he could have hoped for.

He asked everyone to step away from the three vans.

One of the marines brought him three stones from outside of the hangar.

Bram threw a stone at each of the vans and three colored flashes occurred.

The General asked if it was the same technology that was being used at the house.

Bram said that it was but with the difference being in how the protective envelope traveled with each van. Bram went over to the vans but before reaching out to the van he threw a nickel at it and then picked the nickel up and opened the back of the van to show a small box at the corner of the van. He said that it was the coordinate locator that was monitored by the bubbles that generated the laser beam.

One of the break throughs was the greatly reduced size of the bubbles as well as the increase in laser power. He commented that each vehicle took four bubbles to maintain the screen. He used a laser pointer to point to approximately where the bubbles were at the moment. He then opened his computer and commented that the energy used when the shield protected them from the semi had drained the batteries on the bubbles to less than twenty percent. So, the semi attack had actually been a close call.

General Tilman shook his head and said that the military world would love to have the Fold technology.

Bram nodded and said that was one of the things he was really trying to prevent. He felt that the immense power that the Fold capability represented was like the atom and the hydrogen bomb being used together.

The General agreed and said that it was not ready to handle such power.

Chapter 15: Wedding Shield

ɪram and Pat began to spend at least fifty percent of their time on Mataia. She commented that it really helped her to get their home outfitted so it would be in live in condition. She added that the walks on the beach were also quite enjoyable.

The laser barrier had influenced who resided in each house on Mataia. For the first time Pat and Bram were alone together in their own home. It was just the two of them.

The houses on each side and the one directly in back was where their four FBI protectors resided. Mallica had one of the back homes and Erica had the other behind them. The three houses across the street had Linda, Elizbeth, and Lacy living in them.

This put Bram and her in the center of all the homes.

She said that each of their friends had chosen the homes specifically to surround him to ensure they were ready to help if necessary.

Bram replied that he hoped Mataia would be a sanctuary for all of them and that the attacks on Earth would cease now that they had eliminated the future and would soon neutralize Earth in their current time.

She asked if he were ready to get a brief tour of the honeymoon location that she had selected. She took him to a mountain valley that was v shaped with the ocean at the wide part of the V and high mountains on each side and a water stream that meandered leisurely down its center. There were no trees on Mataia, but the blend of grasses and tiny plant like flowers created a stunning view. She said that each day for their weeklong honeymoon, she would like to walk the beach in the early morning and then hike around the valley during the day.

Then at in the evening they would return to their home and enjoy the evening by having dinner that was prepared by Chef D'Carluca and delivered via their Fold technology. She said that all they had to do was to agree on the dinner menu because the Chef had already agreed to do it as his wedding gift.

Bram said that it sounded like a very romantic honeymoon that he was eagerly looking forward to. He commented that being able to return each evening to their comfortable home and have a Chef prepare their meal put a very positive spin on the entire affair.

Pat said that it really did and shared that Linda, Lacy and Mallica were doing something similar, and they all had agreed that on their last honeymoon day they would all dine together at the Mataia Work Center Dining Hall and the rest of their friends would join them. It would be a casual affair that everyone could enjoy.

It would be the first trip out for Chef D'Carluca, and he planned to use the facility on Mataia and prepare a special that he was in the process of inventing. He said that he was thinking of calling it Mataian Delight.

Pat said that she had convince him to let the team have a contest to name the main course after they had all tried it and a prize would be awarded to the winner and to the Chef who had prepared it.

Bram asked how their honeymoon locations would be named.

Pat replied that the honeymooners would get to name them. There would be no prizes, but they would have the joy of having named a specific location on Mataia. Pat added that she and Amy had decided that later the honeymooners would also have the privilege of deciding on the terra forming that would take place in their honeymoon locations.

The day before the wedding Bram took inventory of the various projects and the situation each was in. It became clear that everyone had been working feverishly to get as much done as possible before the wedding.

Each of the projects were hitting their goals with the exception of Lacy's offense team.

Lacy made the point that battling individuals that seemed to command billions of dollars was a monumental task. She called them spoiled fish because they just plain smelled rotten. What frustrated her was that they were very proficient at providing bribes that repeatedly got them off with such a low penalty that it did not matter to them. She had won almost every case but had lost the battle because the penalties were insignificant. She made the comment that having kept them in court as long as she had was the only significant achievement of that effort.

Bram replied that if Lacy traced any attack back to one of her spoiled fish he would be sending that fish as sparklers into the negative realm.

Lacy smiled and commented that he had grown very sharp teeth in dealing with the future.

Bram nodded and replied that he had decided to reduce the risk that those around him faced because of such thoughtless individuals.

Mike called him to let him know that the two fences around the Inn had been erected and was ready for use. Mike said he liked the fact that it had only one entrance gate area that had locks for both the interior and exterior fences.

He said that he and Mary were celebrating their living in a fenced in neighborhood.

Bram replied that he was happy to hear that they approved of the fence. He let Mike know that he would be up to test the laser shield. When he got off the phone, he thought of using the Fold transport but decided against it. He trusted the two to keep such a secret, but it was an exposure that he felt was not warranted. He asked Linda to arrange for a trip up.

Linda said that it would be no problem but suggested that he not create another piece of scrap the size of a semi because there was not much room left in the hangar.

Bram replied that if he did create another piece of scrap he would need to recycle Wheel Two to make room.

Linda frowned and said she was just kidding and that Wheel Two rated to at least be a historic museum piece.

The next day he and Pat both got into the van.

Zoe commented that she was glad that it was her and Eric's turn to guard him during the day. She said that she wanted to see the compound that had been created for the wedding event. And in case of another attack on the vans she wanted to see the shields in action.

She asked when he was going to create a personal laser shield.

Bram smiled and said that he was not sure if he were capable of programing the lasers to create a dynamic shield that moved exactly like the human in it and if it could react fast enough for unanticipated movements.

He ask if Zoe wanted to be the model for the creation of such a program. If she was the model he would call their nose tweaking stand off a draw.

Zoe replied that he was being a little extreme for just a little nose tweaking and that he should use a pig to create the model.

Bram replied that the punishment should fit the crime and using an innocent pig would be inhumane.

The arrival at the lodge brought tit for tat to a close.

Bram had modified the laser shield for the vans so when a door or window was opened, the shield would shut down.

Bram asked Castor to keep all the Marines with the vans and that he lock and guard the outer gate and that Donna lock and guard the inner gate.

Bram led everyone else to the inside of the compound.

He greeted Mike and Mary and thanked them for being willing to go to this extreme.

Pat looked up at the smoking chimney. It was the first time that she had seen it in use. She asked if Mike had an experiment underway.

He smiled and said he wondered if the air inside the shield was able to enter and leave through the shield.

Bram looked at the amount of smoke and said that he had not thought about smoke, but he had been trying to figure out how to keep small animals and birds from getting fried.

He said that Mike's experiment might help him in solving that problem.

He then asked Donna to lock the inner gate and Castor to lock the outer gate and that they both take one step back.

He then energized the laser shield. The red light went on. It was meant to show that the shield was active. It was accompanied by three loud blares.

He and everyone else turned to look at the smoke rising from the chimney.

Pat commented that there seemed to be a few random sparks but most of the smoke made it through the screen.

Mike asked if the fact that some smoke particles interacted with the screen if there might be dust or other things in the air that might be reacting with the screen.

Bram replied that the experiment had given him new insight to the laser screen's interaction with the environment that it was in.

He picked up a stone and threw it up in the air. The stone hit the screen and was vaporized. He asked Donna to do the same along the wall.

He commented that he would have to set up a statistical experiment to learn more about the shields properties.

Castor said he wanted to throw some rocks too.

Bram chuckled and said that all the Marines were welcome to go around the screen and throw stones at the shield. He figured that it was an easy way to test that the shield was complete.

He asked that they check that the red warning lights on the corners were also activated.

Castor let out a "Hurrah" and gave the order to throw rocks.

Bram asked if Mike and Mary minded if they all had a picnic lunch on the veranda. He said that the two of them could try out Chef D'Carluca's version of the Vietnamese sandwich, bánh mì, that had ingredients similar to that of a submarine like sandwich.

Pat explained that the ones they had brought with them was made with the Chef's own crusty bread rolls smeared with pate and mayo, Asian ham as the main protein, pickled vegetables, green onion, cilantro, some fresh chilies as additional garnish. The seasoning was packed separately and was to be drizzled on with a spoon just before eating the sandwich.

Mary said that a picnic sounded great.

Bram deactivated the shield and asked everyone get on the porch.

Castor had the food coolers carried to the porch.

Bram then had Castor lock the outer gate from the inside and do the same with the inner gate.

He then reactivated the screen.

Castor assigned several of the Marines to bring chairs out to the porch and one per cooler to hand out the bánh mì. He made it clear to start with Mary and Mike and then Pat and Bram.

Pat shared that the Chef had packed extra sandwiches because he said that Marines were always extra hungry.

Castor let out a quiet "Hurrah" and said that his first bite of the bánh mì had convinced him that he would have at least two.

Mike said that he would need to learn how to make the sandwich. He would see if the Chef would teach him when he was up for the wedding.

Bram suggested that he get the lessons directly from the Chef who had started making teaching videos that he featured online. He would ask the chef to create a video on how to make his bánh mì. He added that he knew that the Chef had used only fresh ingredients for his bánh mì creation.

The porch scene went quiet as everyone enjoyed their lunch.

When it was clear to Bram that the picnic was over he asked how many sandwiches were left.

Castor looked into the coolers and retrieved six sandwiches.

Pat asked Mary if she would like to have the six.

Mary said that she and Mike would love to have them. They would enjoy them in the next few days.

Mike commented that the sandwiches might be gone sooner than a few days.

Bram then deactivated the shield and green lights came on over the fence gate and at the corners of the fence. He then asked Castor to open each of the gates.

When Castor opened the first gate a physical arm was pulled up as the gate opened and then it fell away from the gate and swung through the space between the fences.

Castor said that he loved that feature, but he still threw a nickel through the gate area before stepping through.

He looked at Bram and said he had learned that trick from a crazy smart scientist.

Bram smiled and replied that it was always smart to be safe versus sorry especially when sorry was to be scattered randomly into negative space.

Mary and Mike waved from the porch and yelled that they would see them all in a week.

On his return he asked Linda to set up a meeting with General Tilman and she should include Castor and Donna in the meeting.

Bram let Linda know that he wanted to find out if the General planned to have a contingent of Marines attend the wedding.

An hour before the end of the workday, Linda escorted the four in.

Bram greeted the General, Matt his aide, Castor, and Donna who followed them in. He let them know that he wanted to understand how his Marine friends were going to protect him and how many would attend the wedding.

He asked Castor and Donna to update the General and Matt about the laser shield. He listened as each of them shared a feature of the enclosure and the invisible laser shield.

He then asked the General what his plans were.

The General said that he was planning on deploying one hundred of his Marines to the wedding.

They would set up camp across the river, but they would be on duty around the lodge twenty-four seven. He also planned to have his attack bubbles on line twenty-four seven.

Bram said that sounded like a good deployment strategy. He then said that he would make sure that all the Marines enjoyed the dinner that would be served at the wedding reception. And just before the wedding they should all gather on the inside of the laser shield where Donna and Castor would manage them.

He asked Castor and Donna to stay a moment at the end of the meeting.

He took out the control for the shield. It looked like a simplified television controller. It was labeled lodge shield. Both buttons were covered. The activate button had a special release cover that needed to be pressed twice to allow it to open. Once the activate button was pressed the cover closed. The cover for the deactivate button could then be flipped open and the deactivate button was available.

Bram showed them a series of similar controllers and said that they would eventually be given to each homeowner, but they had one more feature that during the day that automatically lifted the protective shield up seven feet off the ground to prevent anyone from accidentally walking into the shield.

Castor asked if the two of them could accidentally activate the shield at the lodge.

Bram said that the question was a good one. He said that they would need to be within twenty feet of the fence to be able to activate the shield.

Donna said that made sleeping at night possible. She was deathly afraid of the laser shield and what responsibility of its control implied.

Bram nodded and said he agreed and that he, Remi, and Marcus had worked hard to come up with a way to minimize the risk of mistakes being made by anyone who had access to the controllers. In fact, the risk of someone making a mistake had made them question the activation of the shields for the community.

He said that, currently on Earth, only the shields for his house, for his office, the Viewing Room and now the Rushing River lodge were ever to be activated. Currently he controlled all of them, but he was passing the control of the Rushing river lodge to the two of them. He said that if they accepted he would inform the General.

Castor held the controller up and said that Bram should tell the General that the two them would handle it and say that "they had it."

Bram smiled and said, "hurrah."

Both Castor and Donna replied with a "Oorah" and saluted.

Bram invited them to dinner at this house and suggested they all get a good walk home to help get ready for a dinner that Zoe and Eric were preparing.

Bob and Thomas, who had been silent for the entire time asked if the shield was deactivated so they could safely get out of the building.

Bram nodded and led the way out.

Ron Mueller

<u>Chapter 16: Until Death Do Us Part</u>

Bram had declared the Friday before the wedding a holiday for everyone involved in the wedding party.

Pat had asked all of the wedding party to dinner and had asked Chef D'Carluca to cater the meal but four weddings at once meant that the dinner became quite large and after some discussion, she agreed to have the Stetson family cater the dinner and let the Chef focus on the wedding preparation at the Rushing River Lodge.

The dinner gathering was moved to the recreation center and the Stetsons agreed to cater it.

At dinner Pat asked each of the members involved in the wedding to introduce who they had selected to be part of the Wedding.

Linda said that she had asked Linh and Duong to be the brides Maid and Best man. She shared that Duong had agreed to step in to be best man because Rafael's best friend had spent six months in jail for having gotten into a bar fight and did not get cleared by the FBI because he was currently engaged in a civil trial. She thanked Duong for being willing to stand in.

Pat said she was sorry to hear about the problem with the friend, but she agreed that Duong was a great stand in.

Lacy said that she had asked LeAnn a long-time friend to be her bridesmaid and had her stand up and say a few words.

Raymond stood up and said that his long-time friend Navy Lieutenant Lee Upton would his best man. He had Lee stand up and say a few words.

Mallica said that she had asked Donna to be the brides Maid and Orlando had asked Castor to be the best man.

Donna and Raymond both stood up, bowed, and then sang out a ditty.

> *Marines are best at everything*
> *Love their weapons, Love to sing*
>> *Love almost everything*
>> *We are brothers, sisters, we are friends*
>> *Now were starting a new trend,*
>> *Guarding weddings, Guarding Weddings*
>> *A new thing, A very new thing*
>> *But Marines are the best at everything*

Bram and Pat both stood and chanted the ditty and waved to everyone to stand and do the same.

Orlando reminded everyone that all the Marines that would be present during the wedding would be in their dress uniform. Their weapons would be at the ready and within reach, but the intent was to compliment the event and not distract from it.

Bram then let them know that Amy would be the Bridesmaid and that he had asked Marcus to be his best man and Remi to be a second.

They had all agreed that Marcus's two kids would be ring bearers for all of them.

Pat added that Zuri would be a bridesmaid to all, and she would walk in with the flower girl.

She added that the color for the brides maids dresses was a dark forest green. The groomsmen would all wear matching dark green tuxedo's with light green hankies. She added that everyone would have a white corsage or bouquet.

She then added that Elizabeth and her current heart throb, Dr Wilkins, Rita, Ted, Marial, and Cedric had all agreed to their roles as mother and father to them all.

Zoc asked Bram if he had put up the laser barrier around the lodge because of premonition.

Bram replied that it had been a premonition but now felt that it was more of a certainty that an attack would occur. He said that the semi-truck attempt at running the vans off the highway was a clear indication that someone was once again providing funding and arms to the local extremists.

The dinner ended with everyone enjoying some dancing and using the recreation center facilities.

Very early on Friday morning a large contingent of Marines escorted the wedding party to the lodge. They would spend Saturday morning transporting a large number of the Fold community to the lodges in the area.

Melisa set up the Fold Recreation center so that the rest of the community would be able to attend remotely.

Bram had thanked her for volunteering to set up the remote viewing. He had also arranged that the wedding reception dinner would be served there as well.

General Tilman had arranged for the Marines to provide additional fire power to set up camp during Friday and then take up positions inside the Fold compound. The contingent protecting the wedding would be assigned around the Rushing River lodge periphery.

Bram requested that the Marines all gather inside the laser shield during the wedding and observe the ceremony via several large screens set up on the veranda. They would then be served the same meal as those inside the lodge.

The order for getting meals had been randomly assigned and the Marines were included in that random scheme. There would be three serving tables to ensure the meals were rapidly made available.

He thanked the General for ensuring that the Marine band was part of the one hundred and that group would get special treatment so that they could enjoy the food and then play the background music and then get everyone to dance.

Bram reminded everyone that the wedding event and reception was going to be a continuous process.

Saturday morning after a light breakfast, the wedding party practiced for the wedding ceremony. The Fold Marine Chaplin guided them all through the ceremony. It was to be a nondenominational ceremony.

The processional was from the side entrance to the dining hall. Elizabeth was the officiant and had a short welcome to everyone present or watching. She would then introduce each couple that was getting married.

She then planned to address all four couples and give them the same message of their marital responsibilities.

There would be no readings. It would flow straight to exchanging vows. The four couples had agreed on one vow that they would all say together.

"I am your soul mate and will support you for our lifetime. I will treat you as I wish to be treated. We will have each other's back. The simple gold band that I place on your finger symbolizes the circle of life that we will share."

Then the Chaplain would say a simple prayer and wish them prosperity and a continually growing bond.

The recessional would be a short walk the length of the lodges gathering room and then each couple and wedding party would go to their table where their meals would be served.

Then the food serving lines would be activated and everyone would help themselves to the same meal that the wedding party was enjoying.

Bram commented that he liked the simplicity of the ceremony.

Mary and Mike commented that they liked the fact that Chef D'Carluca was the one that had prepared the enormous amount of food that would be served, and that Stetson Catering was providing the personnel to serve the food.

After the practice, Pat said they had a short time before the actual ceremony began and they should all take a break and then get dressed.

Orlando commented that Castor was getting very proficient at leading the Marines assigned to the wedding protection detail.

He had gotten them all into the compound early and had put the laser shield up. He led the way out to the veranda where General Tilman was welcoming the Marines to the wedding. The General threw a nickel at the screen where it flashed out of existence. He commented that they were all safe and under the guard of one Bram Nielson who on this day would formally wed his soul mate that all of them knew as Pat.

Negative Fold

He smiled and said that Pat had become as good as "Lieutenant" Orlando Gutieres at coming up with ditties. He held up a piece of paper and said he had one that she had written for her wedding day.

He handed the ditty to Orlando and asked him to lead the troops through it several times.

Orlando stepped forward and like an Orchestra leader led the Marines through the ditty. They were loud enough that everyone at the wedding not only heard it but joined in on chanting it.

> *It's Bram's wedding on this day.*
> *Hey, Hey, It's his wedding, let out a loud hurray.*
> *Won't let threats get in the way.*
> *Plans to marry a girl named Pat*
> *She's the girl that's got his back.*
> *We ask who out there stands in his way.*
> *"Lieutenant" Orlando Gutieres says.*
> *It's his marriage day today.*
> *He stands at ready, to pass the test.*
> *Linda and now more than her best friend*
> *Rafael will wed as well along with the rest.*
> *Those objecting are no fun, they better run*
> *For Bram has planted a surprise.*
> *And there will be no compromise.*
> *Cause General Tilman wants some fun.*
> *No compromise, but a surprise.*
> *Run, Run, Run, Cause the General wants his fun.*

Bram gave Pat a hug and said that he really liked her ditty.

The Chaplin called the wedding to order and the Marine band played the bridal chorus."

The flower girl and the ring bearer led the way. The rings were handed to the Chaplin, so he could give them to each couple during the ceremony. All the rings were the same plain gold band but made to fit the fingers of each couple.

The four brides were escorted in by four Marines in their dress uniform and led to the altar that had been set up at the end of the large common area.

The four grooms all had broad smiles on their faces and took the hands of their brides when the Marines lifted it to them.

The Chaplin wed each couple and had just uttered the words asking if there was anyone that objected to the marriages when four successive explosions rock the Inn and literally knocked everyone off their feet.

The General could be heard giving orders to seize the perpetrators of the attack.

He then turned to Bram and asked if there was a way to let his Marines out.

Bram shook his head and asked the Chaplin to finish the wedding and that the attack had been by those who objected to the wedding, but they did not count.

The Chaplin smiled and declared the four as husbands and wives and they should kiss to seal the deal.

After a long kiss, Bram turned to the guests and said that it was time to eat, dance and party.

Negative Fold

He walked over to General Tilden and asked if they were going to have some live attackers to question and find out where they were getting their weapons.

The General said that he had eyes on their prize. He had instructed his Fold bubble offense team to follow each truck that had served as the drone launch pads and he had three helicopters following behind but staying out of sight.

He planned to bring all the people in the trucks to the Fold compound and interrogate them. He figured they were the triggers that had launched the very sophisticated drones, but he wanted the person or persons above them. He was determined to hand those names to Bram and together they would find the people with the money.

He commented that Bram seemed to have a way to make those folks disappear.

Bram asked that when the General had those that had been the fingers on the trigger he would like to get involved in interrogating them.

He smiled and said that he would hold them in their cells until his honeymoon was over.

Bram then went to his wedding table and enjoyed the Chef's wedding day special.

Pat announced that there was a contest to name the wedding day special created by the Chef D'Carluca and that all guests could enter and that the prize would be a thousand-dollar shopping spree at the store that the winner chose.

The prize to the Chef was that his creation would be entered in the contest of his choice, and she would cover all expenses associated with him attending such an event.

There was a cheer from those physically at the wedding and a similar one at the Fold recreation center.

Bram took Pat's hand and led her out to the dance floor area for the first dance.

The Marine band played a cha-cha and he and Pat put on a show.

Orlando immediately threw out a ditty as he led Mallica out to the dance floor.

> *Not only smart.*
> *Finds a beautiful woman right at the start.*
> *Takes her out for lifelong romance.*
> *Not only smart but knows his part*
> *Dance, Dance, Dance.*
> *Romance, Romance, Oh! Sweet Romance.*
> *Not only smart, A beautiful woman from the start.*

Bram laughed and asked if Orlando was making ditties about himself.

A few moments later Zuri came to his table and asked Bram to dance with her.

Bram obliged and they went on the dance floor and danced a tango. It was clear to him that Zuri had been taking dance lessons and she saved him a couple of times when he faltered, and she put on a solo display and then returned to him.

They then danced a waltz and Bram bowed out as one of the young Marines tapped on his shoulder and asked for the dance.

Pat congratulated Bram on having kept up with their miracle young woman.

Bram nodded and replied that it was hard not to cry as he watched the very beautiful Zuri out on the dance floor. He commented it was hard to recall her condition when they first met when she was wheelchair bound.

Pat put her hand on Bram's and said that she too was still in awe at the transformation that the Fold process had on Zuri. She said that she, Elizabeth, and Zuri's mother had spent many hours talking about the miracle transformation. They all agreed that no matter what other amazing things the Fold process would expose, none would ever match the transformation of Zuri from a deformed body to one that was healthy and beautiful.

Bram nodded in agreement.

The General came to their table and complemented Bram and Pat on their dancing and noted that Zuri was attracting all the young single men. He pointed to the young Marine that was dancing with her at the moment and said that the two had now been dancing with each other for at least a half dozen dances and it appeared he had a Marine that was captivated and maybe a Zuri who was as well.

He then said that he had the three drivers of the trucks and three accomplices that were passengers in the trucks. They had spotted a dark green pickup standing in the forest and had followed it back to Seattle.

There the green pickup went to a parking lot and two people got out and went to their vehicles. The bubbles were able to follow each to their homes. He had a local Marine contingent on the way to take them into custody and whisk them to the Fold compound. He said this stretched the legal limits, but he did not want to get any outside law enforcement involved.

They would have nine people and their computers and phones and would figure out who they were in contact with. The General commented that he would let the men sit in their cells and wait to interrogate them until after Bram returned from the honeymoon. He added that Lacy would also be back from her honeymoon and would be able to follow through on any financial connections.

Bram thanked the general and said that when he returned they would pursue the matter right to the financial backer and then they could decide what to do.

Pat signaled the other brides, and they all grabbed their new husbands hands and said that it was time to leave the reception.

Bram collapsed the laser screen and Castor, and Donna opened the gate.

This time Donna was the one to throw a nickel past the gate.

Pat walked to the second black van and got in after Zoe and Eric got in the back. There were four vans to transport the wedding party back to the compound.

Bram had prepared two twelve-person Fold transports. Both would Fold to Mataia for the honeymoon.

<u>Chapter 17: Ether Trail</u>

All the honeymoons were on Mataia. Each was a separate event and took place at the locations selected by each couple. They had all chosen to use their homes in Einstein City as the place to stay at night but to spend each day at their honeymoon destinations.

The honeymoon came to a close at the catered dinner prepared by Chef D'Carluca who had Folded to Mataia.

It turned out that the Chef had come up with a totally vegetarian dish that he had prepared from the plants that he had gathered around Mataia. The spices and a few of the ingredients were from Earth but he named the dish Mataian Lover's Delight. This time he said that he was in the right place and that the dish was a delight to prepare.

Pat complimented him on the ingredients, the wonderful taste of everything. She told him that he had surpassed himself in his inventiveness.

Chef D'Carluca smiled and said that she had provided him with his dream kitchen, and he was going to relish preparing meals on Mataia. He asked if Mataia was going to remain without the animals that provided the meats that he used in many of his dishes.

Pat replied that she and Amy were in the process of terraforming Mataia, but it would be years before Mataia would be providing many of the ingredients that he used. However, he would be able to Fold all the ingredients that he currently used from Earth.

The dinner conversation focused on the wonderful honeymoon experience each of them had. Each couple had taken video pictures and shared the location where they had spent each day of their vacation.

Lacy and Linda and their husbands had spent two nights camping in their honeymoon locations and the rest of the time they had also returned to their houses in what they were all referring to as the "Einstein City" suburbs. They commented that they were going to have to develop star maps and name the different constellations that they had observed.

Bram replied that doing so could be a lifetime naming contest that he was sure his new wife would be willing to organize.

Mallica said that she already had three constellations named. Two of them would be the Castor-Orlando Twins because the two seemed to be guarding a third constellation that she thought should be named the Bram Boiling constellation. She then showed the three constellations on the large screen.

Everyone laughed and said that she had hit the nail on the head. They all agreed that she had named the first three constellations and had won the first contest.

Pat said that she could have two servings of the dessert.

Mallica laughed and said that she was expecting a much larger reward for being the first winner and was going to take three servings.

The next morning, they all got in the same Fold transport and Folded back to Earth.

The General, Marcus, Remi, Lori, and Erica were all in the hangar to greet them. After all the hugging and greetings, the General suggested they meet and discuss how to proceed with the men that they were holding.

Lacy suggested they use the Viewing Room to organize the interrogation process.

Bram agreed and asked that Remi and Marcus join them because they might be able to use the control they had in their ability to view events both in the past and future. He said they could check the truthfulness of the answers that their captives gave to questions that were asked.

Marcus commented that Bram was adding a new twist to the use of the negative Fold environment.

Bram nodded and said that one of the jobs they had was to think through how to set the guidelines of how the negative Fold capabilities should be used but for the moment he was making the call.

General Tilman said that he could think of a dozen ways that the military would want to use that capability. He commented that he did not think that the world was ready for that capability to be in any military hands.

Bram agreed and said his fears were how the military, political and financial organizations would each use the Fold capability. It was beyond what he could imagine.

Lacy suggested they focus on interrogating their attackers. She said she would be pleased to be part of the team that set the guidelines for negative Fold capabilities but at the moment she wanted to nail the perpetrators that had tried to disrupt her wedding.

Bram asked Marcus to get setup to calculate negative Fold coordinates and Remi to Fold observation bubbles.

He asked the General how he wanted to proceed with the interrogation.

The General responded that there was an interrogation room at the holding area that they could use. He thought that Matt should do the questioning. He said that the three of them could be in the observation room and could feed Matt the questions. He commented that their captives had not been exposed to anyone, but their Marine guards and they were to the point where if they were going to talk they would do so with just a little pressure.

Bram asked Lacy how that sounded.

Lacy suggested they make sure that Marcus and Remi were prepared to also send observation bubbles out to locations where the big shots might be located. She finished by saying that she would have preferred a Russian style approach of beating the answers out of their captives.

Bram hugged her and said he understood her resentment but that his mother always said that "you can catch more flies with honey than with vinegar."

Both Remi and Marcus said that deploying the bubbles would be no problem.

Bram noted that a Marine was sitting at some equipment and was adjusting the screen in the room and talking to Matt to get the volume set. He commented that the interrogation room was a little daunting in its emptiness and the observation room seemed to be set up to be relaxing.

The General agreed and said that Matt had on the Marine field uniform to make him seem a little more dangerous. His holster held a fake weapon, and it was intended to be seen by the person being questioned so they would feel intimidated.

Bram nodded and said that now they needed to give Matt a good set of questions.

The General took out a sheet of paper with a set of questions on it.

The first question was to ask the person how they preferred to be addressed.

The subsequent questions on the list were:

> What is your age?
> What sports in High School did you play?
> Who had hired you?
> Had they launched the drone?
> How much were they being paid?
> Who was putting up the money?
> Where had they picked up the drones?
> Who had armed the drones?
> How was the launch timing determined?
> How were the target coordinates determined?

Bram said that the set of questions seemed adequate. He asked Matt if the questions were in the order that he thought was about right.

Matt responded that they seemed to be. He asked if Marcus and Remi would be able to verify the answers in real time?

Marcus answered and said that Matt should give him a signal when a question was important enough to check out and he would give Matt a heads up about the verification launch and then give him what had been learned. He suggested that Matt go slowly through the questions and fill in with conversation when he wanted verification to a question to take up time to allow the search.

Matt said that he would be a sympathetic homeboy and pretend that he had a similar background to the person being questioned and then spin many of the tales that his teacher, Orlando had used on him.

Bram suggested that Matt remove his Marine insignias so he would look less elite while still looking dangerous.

Matt nodded and took off all the pins and shoulder insignias.

Bram said that they should get started and they should go in reverse order of importance of the individuals, passenger seat persons first and drivers second.

Then they should question those who had been in the pickup truck last but also passengers first. In the pickup truck they should begin with the passenger in the back seat then move to the passenger in the front passenger seat and finally the driver.

Lacy said that when a person being questioned seemed to have some sort of extra knowledge she might throw in a question that popped into her mind.

Matt said that he would be ready for any side questions that might pop up.

Bram was impressed with Matt's easy and seemingly friendly questioning approach. The persons that had been in the passenger seats were not very useful in getting information. It was clear to him that they had been more or less clueless helpers who had been attracted by what they saw as easy money.

They were done quickly, and it was time to deal with the drivers.

The tone changed when the questioning of the drivers began.

The first one looked around and asked where the other interrogator was. He took a lunge at Matt who stepped in and stomped on the lungers foot and then physical put him in the chair and shackled his hands to the table.

The driver threatened to sue Matt.

Matt laughed and asked if he understood where he happened to be and if he wanted to live long enough to grow old.

The attitude changed.

But other than having been attracted by the money and willingly deliver the missiles and then drive away with the empty heavy-duty flatbed trailers they were not very useful in learning who was doing the ordering and preparation.

They did learn the pickup point location where each of them had been recruited and would be able to dig deeper at a later time.

They had learned from the delivery drivers that the drones had come ready to fire and all the drivers needed to do was to position the trucks and call in that they were in position. The rest was handled remotely.

Bram then asked Matt to go very slowly with the three that had been in the pickup.

Matt went slowly and methodically in the final session of the three in the pickup truck. It was clear that the three were not answering in a truthful manner. They were not revealing any useful information.

Bram suggested that they take a break and figure a way to get more information from the three.

During the break Marcus suggested that they show the three some pictures of their families at key events like they did for the attacker in the future. He wondered if it would have the same effect on the three and get them to open up.

Bram supported that idea and asked Marcus to get the information as quickly as possible.

Marcus suggested they reconvene after lunch. He figured that by then he would have all the materials.

Bram invited Matt and the General to take a walk around the compound and noodle the approach they would take during the afternoon.

He shared with them that in dealing with the attacker from the future they had taken pictures of his family members at key moments and then put them on the kitchen table. The pictures had triggered the attacker to call the person he was working with.

He shared that after lunch Marcus would have key pictures of each of the men in the pickup at some key event in the past and pictures of wives and children that they would share with the three drivers and then ask them the same questions again.

The General asked how difficult it was to get such pictures.

Bram said that Marcus seemed to have developed a lot of expertise at getting the pictures, but he was not sure how difficult finding information on the men in the pickup would be.

After lunch Marcus came into the cafeteria with a folder. He said that he had mixed news and thought they should meet and discuss what he had found.

Bram suggested returning to the interrogation observation room and Marcus could share what he had.

Marcus said that he had three different results, and each seemed to provide a different amount of leverage.

He said that the guy who had tried to attack Matt had warrants out for his arrest in three states. Two of the warrants would mean misdemeanor charges but one state had a warrant out for an assault and battery that would mean at least ten years in prison.

He commented that the assault warrant seemed like the best leverage, but this guy had also stonewalled answering questions in previous arrest interviews. He was a veteran liar and troublemaker. He had driven the pickup.

He suggested that he preferred turning him over to the state issuing the warrant that would lead to the ten-year prison sentence unless they needed his information.

The front seat passenger in the pickup truck was a friend of the driver and had been in multiple bar fights at a local bar that they often frequented. He added that he was a family man but one who drank too much and gambled. He was rather in a deep financial hole to the bar owner.

He had accepted the job as a payoff of his debt. He believed that he would be clear and away from the grips of the gambling ring but in fact the Boss had commented that they had a sheep in their fold. So, it would be a surprise to that man that he had been duped into believing he would be free from his past mistake.

The youngest of the three, seemed to be an ordinary guy. His car and the grocery cart with the food he had purchased were reported to the local police. One of the checkout clerks remembered checking him out. He and his daughter were joking about the cereal they were buying. The clerk said that the two seemed to be relaxed and enjoying themselves.

Marcus commented that the two seemed to have been abducted in the parking lot.

Marcus said he had figured out how to find her and had verified that the daughter was alive. He had deployed an observation bubble to the site where she was being held and had a bubble standing by with Donna and Castor ready to Fold into the room where the girl was being held. He looked at the General and Matt and said that it would be their call.

The General commented that he wanted to send additional Marines in to take the whole building and asked if Marcus knew how many people were in the building.

Marcus said that the place was a drug house used as a laboratory to synthesize drugs.

The girl was being held in one of the ingredient storage rooms. The two people guarding her were in the hallway outside of the room. She was sitting quietly looking through a book.

He pointed out that they would be able to Fold in and out without disturbing the two in the hallway.

He suggested they inform the police department and let them take care of the rest of the drug house. He made the point that the Marines did not need to be exposed to the drugs.

Matt spoke up and said that he thought Marcus should get the girl out as soon as possible and bring her to the compound. He would use her to get whatever information that her father knew.

Marcus figured that they would be able to get two of the three to provide whatever information that they had.

Matt said that he felt they should begin with deploying Castor and Donna and then bring the girl's father into the interrogation room.

He said that he would get that person to talk.

Bram agreed and said that Donna and Castor should bring the daughter to the detention center and have the doctor check her over. He also suggested that they give her the meal of her choice and get her to feel safe.

The General got on his phone and talked with both Donna and Castor. He told them to get the girl out and if possible to do it like ghosts. He chuckled and said that he knew that the Ghosts were Army, but he wanted the two to be ghosts in action not Ghosts with a capital G.

Bram heard Castor reply and say they would have her out safely in five.

The General replied that they had thirty seconds and hung up.

Bram smiled and complemented the General for having given the Army some recognition.

The General grunted and said that he just had a weak moment, but he was over it.

Matt was surprised when less than a minute later the General answered his phone.

The General put his phone in speaker mode.

They all listened as Donna explained that they had Folded back to the hangar because they had made the call that the girl should be taken to the doctor, be given a shower as well as something to eat.

She said the girl was the same size as one of the girls in the community and she had asked Melisa to bring over a plain but fresh outfit.

Castor said that they would then bring her over to the detention center.

The General smiled but in gruff voice said he would have to talk to both of them later about stretching his orders.

Once he hung up he looked around and said that he wanted to give the two a hug but thought it might be inappropriate and ruin his image as being tough.

Matt shook his head and said that the General's toughness index was pretty low, and he should just go ahead with the hug. Matt smiled and added that of course if he did do the hugging the whole compound would learn about it via a Castor or Donna ditty.

Bram looked at Marcus and asked how he would react if he were the person being questioned and it was his daughter that had been kidnapped.

Marcus immediately answered that unless he got to hug his daughter, he would refuse to answer any questions.

Bram nodded and said he thought as much. He suggested a delay in doing the questioning until Donna and Castor brought her over to the detention center.

He called Pat and asked if she could join Donna and Castor at the Doctor's office. He explained the situation. He had his phone on speaker mode as Pat answered that she and Amy were walking there as they talked. They would stop at the gift shop and get a couple of things.

The General complemented Bram in activating the tough love section of the Marine Corps.

Bram smiled and said that he was using a phrase that he had learned from his mother about using honey and he had the Marine version of honey on the way.

About a half hour later Castor came into the viewing booth and said that he had come in for his chewing out but before that started he wanted to report that a beautiful young girl surrounded by a flock of women were in the meeting room across the hallway.

The General smiled and complimented Castor on doing his job exceedingly well.

Castor snapped to attention, saluted, and replied, "Bamcis." He then said, "follow me."

Bram was the first to follow. He was not surprised to see Pat on one side and Amy on the other side of the young girl. They were carrying on a conversation with her. Melisa and Donna were sitting across the table from them and were also chatting with the young girl.

The room went quiet as the General came in. He looked around and then at Bram and commented that he thought it was his job to explain to him what was going on.

Bram asked that girl her name.

She smiled and said that she was Orianna.

Bram asked if she knew her name meant morning sun.

Orianna stopped for a moment, blinked her eyes, and said that her mother had told her that all the time and added that she missed her mother.

Bram nodded and said that it was hard to lose a mother, but she seemed to have a good dad.

Orianna said that he was the best and she asked if Bram knew where he was.

Bram replied that he did and that she would soon be able to give him a hug.

He turned to Matt and asked if he were ready.

Matt nodded and turned and led the way out of the meeting room.

Marcus commented that he felt that they should somehow figure out how to get this guy away from the drug gang and to a place of safety.

Bram said that he agreed but they would wait to see how he cooperated before deciding how to help him.

They were all in the viewing room when Orianna's father was led in.

Matt began by asking for his name.

The young father answered that he was Ethan Alexander and was thirty-four years old.

Matt turned on the screen and showed the shot of Ethan's daughter in the drug house.

Ethan muttered a curse and asked how Matt had gotten that shot.

Matt replied that he could not share that information. He then showed the shot of everyone in the nearby waiting room.

Ethan asked if it was real.

Matt replied that it was and asked if Ethan was assured of safety for he and his daughter, would he be willing to help them find out who was behind the attack using the cruise missiles.

Matt said that he wanted to give his daughter a hug first to make sure it was all real. Then he wanted to know how Matt could provide them safety. After that he would be an open book and share the little that he knew.

Marcus commented that he had spent his time going back through Ethan's history and found that he was a very reputable person before they had kidnapped he and his daughter. If Ethan shared times and locations, they would be able to get the details and then follow the ether trail to the source giving the order.

Bram asked what skill Ethan possessed.

Marcus replied that he was involved in the sale of defibrillators and a line of pap machines manufactured by a leading manufacturer.

Bram put in a quick call to Melisa and asked her if she could use a person with sales skills. He was not surprised to learn that she would take as many people as he would provide.

He let Matt know that they would offer a job in the Fold compound to Ethan if he volunteered to help.

Matt nodded.

He told Ethan that he was having his daughter brought to him for a hug, then it would be time for Ethan to share what he knew.

He ended by saying that those in power had also authorized him to offer Ethan employment in their secure compound if he participated in earnest to capture the perpetrators of the attack.

Ethan nodded and said he would love to participate in taking out that had kidnapped he and his daughter.

The door to the interrogation room opened and Orianna rushed into his arms.

In a whisper, Bram suggested they all relax for a few minutes and then let Ethan know that at the end of the interrogation, he and Orianna would be taken to an apartment where they would spend the night and that on the following day Orianna would be looked after while he returned to work with them on tracking down the bad guy.

Matt nodded and commented that he was happy to see Orianna safely in her father's arms.

Ethan continued to hug Orianna as he looked at the glass behind Matt and said thank you. He went on to say that he was all theirs. He owed them his daughter's and his life because he would not have survived losing both her mother and her.

Matt stood up and said that interrogation was over and that Ethan and Orianna would be taken to an apartment for the night and dinner could be ordered in to the apartment. There would be a guard on watch but just to provide security. He would be picked up on the following morning after Orianna was taken to school.

Bram suggested that they split the remaining interrogation up. He would work with Ethan in the office area Viewing Room on the following morning and get him to share his information there.

Marcus would stay in the interrogation viewing room and work with both Matt and he in parallel.

He said it would be easy for him to be versatile with time if Marcus needed to help Matt make progress.

He said that he had a good feeling about Ethan. He asked Melisa to be with them in the Viewing room and chat with them in a sort of informal interview.

Matt chuckled and accused Bram of picking the sweet apple and leaving both a spoiled one and a sour one for him to cook with.

Bram wished him good luck and that he was available for any consultation Matt might want. He reminded Matt that he had pulled him back from drowning in the sea but that he still expected him to cook on his own.

Matt let out a "Hurrah" and said that he was ready to cook.

The General let out a "Hurrah" and said he was ready to be the fry cook and singe the remaining butts that refused to cooperate.

Bram replied with a "Hurrah" and said, "lets attack."

Chapter 18: The Good and the Bad

Ʊhe next morning, Bram had Ethan and Orianna brought to his house. Pat greeted them and asked if Orianna would enjoy some pancakes smothered in butter with Maple syrup for breakfast.

The breakfast was rather quiet, and Bram preferred it that way. He had invited Melisa to join in and then walk with him into work.

After breakfast he led the walk to the office Viewing Room. He listened as Melisa chatted with Ethan as she did a walking interview.

He was not surprised to hear Ethan ask if Melisa was the good cop establishing his profile. He said he was OK with it but said he had not prepared for her subtle approach.

Melisa replied that she was checking him out to see where he might fit in the organization when Bram gave her the word.

Ethan asked her if it was Bram that ran the place.

Melisa replied that there was an official program manager, but Bram was the person who guided them all.

Ethan and Orianna were holding hands as they walked, and he bent down, and he asked what she thought of everyone so far.

Orianna squeezed his hand and replied that everyone had been super nice. She thought that Mom would approve of everyone. She looked around and commented that there were a lot of people walking with them and there was a helicopter flying over them. She asked why they were all around them.

Bram looked over his shoulder and said they were afraid that he would trip and fall. They were there to pick up the pieces and put him back together.

Orianna laughed and said that he didn't act or look like a humpty dumpty.

They arrived at the entrance to the office area and Bram led the way to the Viewing Room and it was time to see how helpful Ethan might be.

Linda had followed them, and she asked what she could do.

Bram asked her to order in refreshments and then show Donna and Orianna to a huddle room where they could enjoy playing a game or reading. He asked Castor to remain in the Viewing Room. He asked Zoe and Eric to go with Orianna and see if she knew any games they could all play. He knew that Bob and Thomas would remain, and he asked them to sit with Ethan.

Ethan said he played competitive chess, but he was not going to challenge Bram to any game because he hated loosing.

Bram smiled and replied that he knew every chess move but he had a much bigger and more complicate board that he now played on where staying alive was the reward.

He asked whether Ethan was ready.

Ethan nodded and was starting to apologize about not knowing much.

Bram stopped him and asked him to only answer questions. He then asked the location of where he had been approached by the drug dealer.

Ethan said he was coming out of the grocery store when he and Orianna were stopped at gun point and told to get into an old decrepit van.

Bram asked for the date, time, and location of the grocery store.

Ethan had the date and location then he stopped to think about the time. He said that it was after picking up Orianna from school, so he figured that it had to be around three forty-five or so. He was going to ask a question, but Bram again put up his had to stop him.

A moment later Marcus said he had it and the scene came on the screen.

Ethan began to utter a curse but stopped. His eyes seemed glued to the scene as it unfolded.

Bram asked if the scene was how Ethan remembered it. He then asked, "do you know where they took you?"

Ethan shook his head and said that they put a hood over both of their heads. He said when the hood came off he was standing in a room looking at a person that he figured was the leader of this gang, but Orianna was nowhere in sight.

Bram spoke to Marcus for a moment and then the screen showed Ethan standing with his wrist zip tied behind his back standing in front of a rather well dressed and handsome drug dealer who was leaning back in a very large business desk chair. He was wearing sunglasses and smiling. He stood up and came around the desk and patted Ethan on the cheek and then asked if Ethan wanted his daughter back alive or in little pieces.

Ethan ask what he possible could have that was valuable but yes he wanted his daughter back alive.

Bram panned the room and took in three other people. He got clear shots of their faces and then asked Ethan if he knew any of their names.

Ethan shook his head and said he didn't even know the bastard that was the boss.

Bram replied that he was not the boss of much. He ran a meth lab and a few drug pushers. The bigger fish simply collected a percentage of the take.

They all listened as the drug dealer said that the boss had received a call from his boss in Miami and told him to find a patsy at random and coerce that patsy to push a button when he was instructed to do so. For doing so whoever was with him at the time of pickup would be allowed to live.

Bram asked if that was how Ethan remembered it.

Ethan nodded but it was clear he was speechless.

Bram said that later everything would become clear, but Ethan should hang in and continue to answer questions.

After they left, the leader dialed the phone. Bram asked if Marcus had the number and who it belonged to.

While they were waiting they listened to the conversation and learned that Orianna was to be kept alive as a potential bargaining chip, but she was on the chopping block if it became clear that she would not be needed. The boss on the phone went on to say that her dad was dead meat walking.

Ethan shook his head and commented that his arrest had saved his life.

Bram nodded and said that there were a couple of more scenes he wanted him to see.

Ethan had a hood put over his head and led out the back and put into a van. They followed the van to a warehouse area where Ethan was taken out of the van and the zip tie cut off. He was told to count to twenty and then take off his hood. He would be picked up by someone driving a dark green pickup truck.

Ethan took off his hood as the large dark green shiny pickup truck entered the parking lot and drove over to him. Two men got out of the truck and walked toward him. They asked if he was expecting to be picked up.

Ethan responded that he was.

The driver handed him a small black controller that had a red cover over a button.

The driver held up a similar one and so did the second person. He said that they were all being held hostage and unless they pressed the button when they were told to do so they or someone they loved would be killed.

Bram asked Marcus if Matt was seeing the three in the parking lot.

Marcus replied that Matt had been waiting until he had some sort of information that would give him an idea of how to continue the interrogation.

Matt came on and said that he saw the two.

Bram suggested that they follow the truck back in time to the point where the driver first got in to begin the journey to see if they could pinpoint the moment when he got enrolled.

Marcus did a great job doing a series of Folds back in small enough increments that it looked like they were following the truck as it drove backward. The truck backed into the Turtle Bar and Grill, the driver, and the passenger both got out and walked backward past the bar and to a room located at the end of the bar. Marcus took several large steps in time to the point where the two were escorted in and faced the person sitting at the desk.

They then listened as the two were told that their hefty bar bills would be erased, and they would get an additional ten thousand dollars for simply pushing a button.

Negative Fold

The driver asked what the buttons activated and was told not to ask and once the buttons were pushed the controllers were to be trashed.

Bram asked Marcus to go back to when the Bar owner got the call and when the controllers were delivered.

A few moments later Marcus came back on and on the screen they could see and listen in on the call. The bar owner was talking to a person in Miami and replying yes sir, yes sir I can find the right guys. They heard the Miami boss saying that each of the two would get one hundred thousand dollars and the Bar owner saying he could definitely get the right guys at that level of compensation.

Bram asked Matt whether that might give him some leverage with the two. He pointed out that the questioning might not be needed since Marcus had the phone number and would soon have the location.

The Miami connection was the in the same building as the one they had gotten from the drug dealer, but it was a second person in Miami. Bram speculated they were sharing the risk but most likely there would be one major money trail.

Lacy spoke up and said that both of the persons on the Miami end were on her list. They both took money from her main suspect and did dirty jobs, such as bribing folks or threatening them. She said that they needed to take one more step and intercept the request to the two.

Marcus said he was ahead of them and had followed one of them to a meeting in a limo that took place in a parking lot.

Bram and everyone in the Viewing Room watched as Marcus took a tiny camera bubble through a gap in the limo driver's side window and was able to get a clear shot of the back seat area. They watched as the controllers were handed over with the explanation of how they should be handled.

Bram asked Marcus to find the coordinates of the person in the back seat in current time.

He let Marcus know that he was ending his meeting and was then going to the lab.

Once he was off the phone with Marcus, he asked Ethan if he wanted to work as a travel agent in Melisa's travel agency.

Ethan asked if the work was in the protected compound.

Bram replied that it was and if he were interested in the job he should give her a call and volunteer to work for her. Bram said that the two of them would discuss the compensation.

Ethan replied that the pay was not as important as knowing that Orianna would be safe. He would only need enough to buy food and pay the rent.

Bram smiled and said that he should also consider being able to save money so that Orianna would be able to go to college.

He then asked Castor to get Ethan and Orianna a ride to their apartment.

He asked Matt to turn the driver of the pickup over to a Texas ranger since that person had an outstanding warrant for manslaughter. He should turn over the second person over to the Montana Highway patrol who was looking for him for causing an accident with a bus were multiple people were injured.

Lacy asked about the billionaire that they had exposed.

Bram said that he would personally handle that situation.

He asked her to handle the drug pusher, the Portland bar owner, and the Miami connection.

Lacy said that she had enough information and would work with Marcus on any loose ends and together they would have all of them sitting in some penitentiary.

Bram left the viewing room and went to the lab where he met Remi.

Remi pointed to the bubble and asked if he needed any help.

Bram pointed to Zoe and Eric and said that the two of them were deadly enough on their own.

Castor commented that he was miffed that he and Donna were being left behind.

Bram smiled and replied that he would be back in a second and they could continue the tit for tat.

He Folded to the coordinates provided by Marcus

He heard Marcus quietly state that he had his back and that he had the billionaires coordinate and Bram only had to Fold him.

Bram Folded into the coordinate of the billionaires office.

The billionaire was standing at the window looking out at the ocean.

Bram walked up, tapped him on the shoulder and when the billionaire turned to face him and he looked him in the eyes, pressed the Fold button and the billionaire vanished.

He had followed his Aikido instructors adage to act first and talk after. Once he had pressed the Fold button he got back into the transport and Folded back to the lab. There on the large screen they all witnessed a small multicolor flare as the billionaire's body met the laser protection screen of the house.

He turned to Zoe and Eric and asked if the Fold had been exciting.

Zoe looked at Castor and said if he thought Bram was fast at the trigger in battle he was even faster when he was Folding someone into the activated laser shield. He was so fast that he said goodbye to the billionaire after he had Folded him.

Bram said that it was time to go home and enjoy dinner and he would concentrate on how they would disappear all the Fold information from Earth.

The End

<u>Ripples in time</u>

<u>Chapter 1: Transition Plans</u>

As the saying goes, all good things must come to an end. It was clear to Bram that it was time to end the presence of the Fold effort on Earth. He had mixed feelings about the ability of everyone making the transition to another planet, in another solar system in another galaxy. Mataia, the destination planet was equivalent to what earth would have been before more than plant life had begun. It was less stressed and had less tectonic plate activity but otherwise it had a similar proportion of water to land mass and the atmosphere was almost a duplicate of what the Earth had.

The ability to Fold between Earth and Mataia had made the transition a reality.

Bram met Eric, Jeffrey, and Elizabeth to discuss the transition of the Fold effort to Mataia. The four of them developed an initial transition plan that was as flexible as possible.

Bram pointed out that it would take several years to fade out the Fold project from Earth in a manner that it would draw no attention. The Fold program had never become public but there were influential individuals who had been aware of it. He pointed out that Olivia Newton a member of the now dissolved Senate Oversight Committee was coming out to meet with him in a desire to be part of the Fold project. He added that he hoped that Jeffrey and she would work together to establish the Mataian government.

Jeffrey smiled and replied that he would love that assignment from his new boss.

Bram shook his head and replied that his head would remain in the world of science in an effort to move the Fold capability forward.

He then asked Erica whether she would lead the move of the Fold project from Earth to Mataia.

Erica nodded and said that she was pleased to be the one to help get Mataia going. She felt that it would be a high point of her work life.

Bram said that his objective was to leave Earth in such a fashion that no one would know they were gone.

Elizabeth spoke up and asked what an old lady like her could possibly do to help make it all happen.

Bram said that she should think about setting up the education system on Mataia. She would need to recruit top talent to be the teachers and instructors of a system that began at the lowest grade and went through to where PhDs were graduating.

Elizabeth asked if there were school buildings on Mataia.

Bram smiled and said that she should get together with Amy and Pat to lay out the buildings and then work with Erica to figure out how to outfit the school system. He added that her question highlighted the monumental undertaking that the move to Mataia represented.

He said that he had done a little thinking on the details but was certain that there would be several areas that he felt would be challenges.

One was the logistical arrangements that were necessary to support a functioning Einstein City. Supplies from Earth would need to be constantly Folded in. He felt that they needed a facility separate from the current Arrival Terminal to accommodate the arrival of the logistical materials.

He went on to point out that there most likely were additional facilities that they had not thought about that would need to be built and then transported to Mataia. He was planning on having Amy and Pat be the two who would lead that effort.

Ron Mueller

The second challenge would be to vet the personnel that would make permanent moves to Mataia. Their selection needed to be carefully considered. They should be vetted as to their love for the work they were currently doing in the Fold project and to seeing a future for themselves in living on Mataia in the long term. He added that for all their lifetimes return to Earth would be possible but at some point, that would become a rare occurrence.

Erica suggested that she spend time with each of the other team members and develop the details of a transition plan. She pointed out that sometime in the future the Fold facility at Dallas would need to be slowly erased. She did not think folding the existing buildings to Mataia would be practical nor desirable because Amy and Pat had improved the way homes and other structures were built for Mataia. However, she pointed out that the homes at the site could be Folded to various countries to establish very nice communities for people needing homes. She thought that the industrial buildings could be relocated to a strategic location where they could continue to be used as part of the logistical material handling facility for things going out to Mataia.

Bram thanked Erica for taking the lead in that area.

He said he wanted to work with Elizabeth and Jeffrey on selecting the personnel that would be emigrating to Mataia.

He added that he also wanted to work with Melisa and Marcus to set up vacation spots on Mataia as well as a way to maintain the Earth vacation spots. He said that he felt that the transition would be much less stressful on everyone if their leisure time could be spent on both planets. In that way, leaving Earth would not be so dramatic.

Jeffrey asked whether the members of the Stetson family were in line to move to Mataia.

Bram shared that he had talked with Lacy and Linda and the two definitely were eager to be included. The rest of the Stetson family were on the fence. They were quite willing to aid in the transition, but they felt that they were going to remain on Earth. Linda had let him know that her brother Luke was eager to set up the transport manufacturing center on Mataia or do whatever was needed. He thought that his future was going to be there.

Bram later met with Pat and Amy to discuss what they thought the transition needed to include.

Amy pointed out that it would take years to slowly change the Mataian environment to at least make it able support life like Earth.

Amy pointed out that they needed to keep everything in balance and that the transition should move slowly forward over their lifetime and perhaps beyond, in short it would take time.

Bram said that he would love to take part in some of the Mataian transformation details of moving as time permitted but they would all be very busy for as far into the future that he could see, and they should continue to default, to taking it slowly and Fold plants and animals to Mataia in a controlled and well managed manner. He added that he was counting on the two of them setting up a team that would manage and oversee that effort.

He then met with Marcus to discuss the transition to work on Mataia.

Marcus said that he was eager to make the move and would plan to work there each day. He needed to get his home there organized. He pointed out that he was taking mini vacations with Mylan and Marcus Jr. on almost all the upcoming weekends for the next several months. He had been outfitting his house on Mataia and had taken one mini vacation there with the two and they were now enthused about the move. The two had really enjoyed the beach that they had gone to and the hike in several of the valleys.

Bram reminded Marcus that there was a naming contest for all locations on Mataia and as well as for naming the stars visible from the planet's surface. He suggested getting the two into those contests as a way to enthuse them about their move. He also made the point that they could move into their new home and still attend classes in Dallas or on weekends do mini vacations on Earth.

Marcus smiled and said that the discussion had solved his concern about their safety at his current home at the Fold housing complex. He would be making the move as soon as possible.

Bram shared that he and Pat had started to live on Mataia and Folding to work in the Morning and that his FBI bodyguards were doing the same. He was hoping all of the inner circle would soon be doing something similar.

He pointed out that doing so had already surfaced several life activities that were not significant but that needed to be addressed as they transitioned.

Marcus asked for an example.

Bram said that setting up the materials and supply chain logistics was the area that had been exposed when they had to take up a supply of toilet paper and paper towels. That simple need had clarified the fact that there were no trees to supply the fiber to make paper. So, both those items needed a replacement or a long-term logistical plan.

Marcus laughed and said that they would certainly have to solve many such weighty and critical problems.

Bram's next meeting was with Mallica in person and Orlando on screen. They discussed getting Mallica focused on working with him on exploring both the positive and the negative Fold environment. He shared that she and Marcus would be central to that effort.

He asked Orlando if he were willing to establish a way to keep order on Mataia.

Orlando commented that he thought he would enjoy such a role.

Bram challenged him to do it in a way that would require no weapons and would fundamentally be based on the philosophy of treating others the way he wished to be treated. He challenged Orlando to make the way to keep order a friendly embrace.

Orlando laughed and asked if he should wear a Santa Clause outfit.

Bram shook his head and said that he wanted Orlando to be the Marine that he was and to see if he could set up a system that would make Zuri proud.

Orlando nodded and in a more serious tone said that he now understood how serious Bram was.

Orlando smiled and said he understood perfectly what Bram expected.

Bram suggested that he enroll Castor and Donna in that effort.

Bram realized that Mallica had tears in her eyes and asked what was up.

Mallica shook her head and commented that she had just thought through all the things that had transpired since hanging on out in the desert compound where they had all started. She was glad that Elizabeth had convinced her to stay on.

Bram nodded and thanked her for staying. He felt bad about that time but felt great about everything that she had contributed. He added that she was a big part of the success of the Fold effort and Orlando was a big part of having kept him alive. They were both more than just his good friends, they were now more like family.

His final discussion for the day was with Remi and Lori.

Remi commented that he was eager to make the move to Mataia and to get his lab functional there. He said he and Lori had reviewed the people in the lab and agreed that they had a group of very hard-working people who were eager to be a part of the continuing Fold effort. The research and analysis of the Mataian environment and any samples that would be gathered from somewhere in the universe would be something they would never be able to experience in any other work environment.

Lori added that she had met with each of their current staff members, and everyone had said they definitely wanted to stay with the Fold effort.

Bram asked the two to work with Pat and Amy to make sure that housing would be available, and that the logistics group be kept appraised of the number making the move.

He commented that the pace of transition was going to be limited by how quickly they could establish a place for everyone to live and to adjust the quantity of materials logistics to support Mataia and to obtain equipment to handle and store the materials.

He said that he would need to make sure that Erika had a handle on world building at a fast forward mode.

That evening he discussed the situation with Pat as they sat on their two person recliners.

Zoe and Eric were having a cup of tea in one set of easy chairs and Bob and Thomas in the other set. In the past only two of the four had been in the office at the same time lately the four had often sat in at one time.

Zoe commented that the four of them had discussed the mountain of effort that faced them all for the move and had decided that they should figure out how to jump in to help and in the short term do whatever was needed during the initial transition.

Bram thanked them and said that they should get with Erica, Amy and Pat and see where the help was needed. He said that he was sure they would be taken up on their offer to help.

Zoe commented that she was excited about the move, but she also wanted everyone to remember that the role of the four was first as the bodyguard for their loveable and zany mad Fold scientist.

Bram said that he hoped that in the near future, they would think of each other only as very good friends.

The next morning Bram asked Linda to see if Ray could join in on the meeting that he was planning to have with Olivia Newton in the afternoon.

Linda smiled and asked if Bram was going to make Lacy's new husband an offer he could not refuse.

Bram smiled and asked if Ray had any legal and organizational skills.

Linda replied that she had no clue how good he might be, but he had impressed her sister enough to marry him and that spoke highly about his character.

Bram said that Lacy's acceptance was good enough for him and yes, he would make him an offer that he hoped was a big enough net to pull him in.

Linda asked if it was OK to share with Lacy that Ray would be in the meeting with Olivia Newton.

Bram said it would be fine, but he did not know exactly what the offer was going to be.

Linda said that any offer would be acceptable, and that Ray had been worried about not being able to get on the Fold staff.

Linda then asked what he might have in mind for Rafael.

Bram asked Linda to give him several suggestions about where Rafael would be most interested in working. Then she could set up a meeting with him so that he could get to know him better. He commented that he had spent time with him before and after the wedding, but they had not discussed work.

Linda smiled and said the Evenders, and the Tailors would be the Stetson replacement on Mataia.

Bram thanked her and said that he wondered when fishing on Mataia would be as good as the Stetsons had shown them in Dallas.

He asked Linda to let him know when Olivia arrived and to make sure there were overnight accommodations ready as well.

Bram then went into his office after Zoe and Eric had declared it clear. He went straight to the bookshelf and opened the tiny door and took Isaac and Ada into his hand and carried them over to his desk.

He asked them whether he should move the boulder in the desert to Mataia and laughed when both of the mice nodded their heads up and down.

Zoe came over and asked whether they should make sure that their father, Einstein, also made the trip. She pointed to them as they bobbed their heads up and down.

Eric asked whether there was a desert-like area on Mataia.

They all looked at each other and said that they could not remember seeing a desert in any of the videos they had seen. Zoe said she would follow up and go searching for the right place to move the boulder.

Bram said that Marial had mentioned that one of the many unexplained artifacts was a large boulder located on one of the few desert islands on Mataia. There seemed to be no explanation of how it had gotten there nor why the island was the only place where mice were the dominant species. He suggested that Zoe look for that island.

Linda buzzed in and said that Olivia would be at his office in fifteen minutes, and she had Ray standing by.

Bram picked up Isaac and Ada and carried them back to the bookcase and closed it after the two went in.

Linda knocked and brought Olivia in.

Bram greeted her and made the point of recognizing Zoe and Eric as part of the meeting. He had Olivia sit next to him at the table and with Ray on the screen across from them.

After introducing Olivia, Bram stated that the objective of the meeting was to establish the leaders of the group that would write the constitution for a new world government.

Chapter 2: Mataia Constitution

*H*is statement was met with silence. It was clear to him that he had surprised everyone in the room.

He looked at Olivia and then over to the screen at Ray and asked if there were any questions.

Olivia asked where he was planning to set up his government. Ray asked if it would be on Earth.

Bram said he was asking them to write the constitution for a world government, for the world of Mataia. It would be the planet that everyone associated with the Fold effort would move to.

Once again Bram was met with silence. He asked Linda to que up the Mataia video.

He then explained what the two were about to see was something that only his inner circle had seen before. They would see a world that had been named Mataia.

The tour of Mataia began and for the next hour they watched the presentation. Both Olivia and Ray would periodically comment on the splendor and the beauty that was shown. At the end, Bram said that they had taken a quick tour around a new world. It was a world located several light years away in a solar system similar to Earth's solar system. This new world would be home to those who were willing to leave Earth and live there.

Bram then turned on the tour of Einstein, City and declared that it was the first city on the planet and was already being used by about twenty of the Fold personnel, including himself. It needs many small items to make it a fully independent functioning city and it would take time to make that happen.

After the brief arial tour Bram stopped and suggested they all get a cup of tea, coffee or other refreshments and then continue the meeting.

While they were getting coffee Olivia asked if what she had just seen was real. She had been blown away when they had gone on the Fold Vacation in Greece but to be shown a full city on another planet seemed to be impossible. How had he achieved it in such a short period of time and how had the buildings been built in such short order? She said she saw no construction equipment or ongoing construction. She commented that it seems so polished and perfect that it was hard to believe.

Bram sat down at the table and nodded and said that he had his team of super people to thank. They had accomplished what she had seen in record breaking time. He went on to share that everything that she had seen was built on Earth and Folded into place on Mataia.

Ray mentioned that Lacy had told him that he would be blown away by what he was going to learn in the meeting.

He knew she had been dying for him to learn more about the Fold effort. She said that he would learn it from Bram or not at all. He asked what he personally had to do to be an integral part of the Fold effort and that he wanted to be as passionate as Lacy was about it.

Bram asked Olivia if she was ready to commit to the Fold effort.

Olivia nodded and said that she had some family-oriented questions before jumping in, but she did want to jump in. She wanted to make sure about the short- and long-term education of her children. She also wanted to know what her husband could do. Finally, she wanted to know how the transition would be handled. How would the family stay connected with friends and other family members?

Bram liked her questions. He made a point that he was working on Mataia during the morning and finishing the day at his office on Earth. Other than having to keep the Fold technology invisible it was in fact no different than commuting to work in the morning and going home in the afternoon.

He said that how one handled the day and how the transition would be handled would need to be tailored to each individual. She would only need to set up an isolated location where she and family could be picked up and then return via Fold. She and family could design the transition as it fit their needs. The only difficulty would be making sure everything was kept secret.

Olivia shook her head and commented that it was hard to grasp the flexibility that was available in going to and returning from a place several light years away. She had not envisioned the Fold capability to the extent that she was now getting exposure to.

She asked why Bram was isolating the Fold capability from the rest of the Earth's population.

Bram shook his head and asked her to think about the impact to the current social, economic, and military situations that she knew about. If she came to a different conclusion and had the means to manage making the Fold capability part of Earth's current situation, he would like to hear about it.

Olivia thought for a moment and said that she did not have a clue how that would be possible.

Bram said that he had come to that conclusion, but he had also asked those on his team the same question and they did not have an answer either.

He shared the fact that the Fold effort had suffered many physical attacks that included military action, rocket attacks from both the current time and had suffered attacks from the future as well.

He pointed out that Fold was a capability that had yet to be fully understood and it was a threat to a reality that everyone had come to believe was fixed but was in fact malleable.

Olivia asked how he was going to manage that from Mataia.

Bram replied that Fold was being disappeared on Earth and he was working on how to put barriers in place that would help contain how Fold got utilized on either planet. He admitted that he was not sure how it would all get done and whether he would be successful. He commented that he had no clue if the attempt to contain and control the Fold capability would be successful.

Olivia said she had one final question and that was how long the transition would take.

Bram replied that it would most likely be longer than any of them would live and that their children or grandchildren would be the ones that would live in a completely independent Mataia.

Olivia said she like the tenor of his answers. She said that she would definitely embrace the effort. She would do her best at creating a government that would last through future generations and would produce a society that focused on embracing and honoring each other.

Bram smiled and said that he looked forward to her leadership and in being part of setting up the Mataian government.

Zoe had expected that Bram would convince both Olivia and Ray to be part of the effort. She had previously had her friend in the FBI do extensive checks on both of them and had been please to find out that they had no blemishes other than some speeding tickets.

She had learned that both of Olivia's kids, though very good in school, were heavy party drinkers. She felt that this would be a risk to the Fold effort.

Ray was the one with the speeding tickets, with the most recent being in the last month.

She spoke up and asked if they could openly discuss a few issues that were personal and involved other family members.

Bram let Ray and Olivia know that he had asked Zoe to dig into both of their personal and family backgrounds. He followed up by saying that he wanted to make this a positive move and not a punitive one.

He suggested that they tackle Ray's issue first and then after that ask him to sign off. They would then address the issue associated with Olivia.

Ray put up his hands and said he was guilty. He shared that he received the official notice of his speeding ticket in the mail just that morning.

Bram nodded and said that he needed to pay off the previous two as well as the one that he had just received. He should figure out how to control his lead foot or risk losing his new job at writing the Mataian constitution and figure out how to live remotely from his wife.

Ray said he would take care of his problem immediately and become a casual driver.

Bram thanked him and said that Erica Wilson would be in touch with him to arrange his transition into the Fold program.

After Ray signed off, Bram looked at Olivia and said that her problem was family oriented, and it was about her two children.

He commented that he had acted just as they were now acting and that it was a growing up phase thing. He wanted to let her know about it so they could figure out how to change the actions that put them at risk.

Olivia had her hands on the table, and they were trembling. She asked if they were into drugs.

Bram said that they were not into drugs, but they and their friends were into drinking too much at the parties they were throwing. This was the issue that they had to address.

He asked where the two were thinking about majoring at in college and what career they were interested in.

Olivia said that she had asked them and had been disappointed that neither had expressed a passion for any particular field and they were more or less at a loss to what they wanted to do.

Bram commented that he had talked with them during the weekend Fold vacation, and it seemed they were very smart.

Olivia replied that both of them got very good grades and were in the top five percent of their class.

Bram asked if perhaps they could get them more seriously focused in an area that would be fruitful for the Fold effort.

Eric spoke up and said that Dennison had expressed his interest in the FBI or in law enforcement. He could be on the team that designed the support and aid force on Mataia.

Zoe said that she had spent time with Angela and had learned that she wanted to design clothes. She might be enticed by setting up a fashion design shop on Mataia that at first imported luxury brands from Earth.

Bram smiled and looked at Olivia and said that it seemed they had two volunteers to engage her children and give them a vision of the future that might help get them to stop their heavy drinking at parties.

Olivia said she would love the help but how would they connect them in a natural way?

Zoe suggested that they use the fact of her new job would require them to move to a new location as a way to get them to come out to Dallas for a visit. While they are visiting, they could stay in the new home that you would be living in. They could meet a couple of the older members kids in the Fold community who are getting ready to go to college. They could be touring the work projects that are underway.

And then Zoe laughed and said that they could go fishing with Bram and be in some really live action.

Olivia laughed and said that it sounded like a good plan, but she wanted them to wear Kevlar vests when they went fishing.

Bram said that he would plan several fishing trips before they went out to make sure his fishing trips had entered a peaceful time frame.

He then declared the day over and that they would all go home and enjoy whatever dinner Bob and Thomas had prepared.

As they walked out, Linda stopped Bram and told him that Lacy had called her up and said that she thanked him for figuring out how to get lead foot Ray to slow down. He had called her and had said that he had paid all his speeding tickets and had ordered a throttle limiter that would prevent him from going more than five miles over the speed limit.

Bram laughed and asked Linda to tell Lacy that he hoped that it would work.

Olivia said hello to Pat as they walked to the van waiting for them. She thanked Bram for inviting her to join them for dinner. She asked what was on the menu.

Bram smiled and said that unless Zoe and Eric knew then it would be a surprise to all of them. Bob and Thomas were doing the cooking, and they always picked a recipe that they wanted to try out and rounded out the main course with salad and some vegetables.

Olivia said that she thought that was a great way to end the day.

Bram agreed and said that all of them, himself included had developed a broad set of meals they liked to prepare. He admitted that he probably had the narrowest set of meals that he periodically prepared, and he mostly did breakfasts and lunches. His meals were weekend ones where he had enough time to cook.

Pat said that Bram had improved over time, but Zoe and Eric were the ones that seemed to come up with the most interesting menu's and that she was just ahead of Bram in meal recipe preparation but not by much.

Zoe said that it was an unfair comparison. She and Eric got the opportunity to search out and cook recipes every other day. They had also gotten recipe help from the Stetson catering group who sent over recipes they thought would be of interest. All she and Eric had to do was to cut down on the ingredient amounts because the recipes were generally for a large number of people. She laughed and said that properly reducing the spicing often led to hilarious results.

Bram agreed that what the two put on the table had to be treated with a good amount of respect. He remembered two times when the spices were overwhelming and one time that he had to ask for the soy sauce and hot pepper. But some of their good meals could rival those of Chef D'Carluca.

Their van drove into the basement. Bram said that he was going to stop a moment in the office and then come up for dinner.

Pat escorted Olivia up the stairs.

Zoe sensed that Bram planned to share something that was on his mind. She and Eric did a thorough sweep of the office. There were no listening or other devices.

They signaled for Bram to enter. His Marine guards waved and backed the van out of the basement.

Bram walked in and sat at the front edge of his desk. He asked how the four of them were taking the move to Mataia and if there was something that he could do to make the transition smooth for them.

Eric replied first and said that he and Zoe had discussed this in length with each other and they had also engaged with Bob and Thomas.

They all agreed that they wanted to take the transition slowly. They would continue to maintain their current protection cycle until they got notice that the assignment was ending. This would allow them to use their FBI contacts to vet people and to check out suspects until the very end.

Zoc added that after that time they would use their knowledge about the system and the help of Linh and Duong to tap into the various systems when they needed to get the information to vet someone.

Bram said that he agreed with waiting until they got the notice that the bodyguard assignment was over.

He said that he would like to be informed when the more clandestine effort was needed. He was sure that they could pull off such efforts, but he wanted to make sure that when such an effort was needed that all the resources would be aligned to the effort.

Zoe nodded and said that the four had discussed exactly the point that Bram had just made.

Bram thanked them and said that they should complement Bob and Thomas for their great support for the expanding work of the Fold program.

Zoe said that there were two complexities that had surfaced during their discussions on the transition to Mataia.

She said that both Bob's and Thomas's remote love affairs had reached a new level, and they were wondering how to handle them.

Bram asked what the barriers to making their romances work might be.

Zoe replied that both of them wanted to have weekends off so they could pursue their romances. They were wondering if they might be able to use two of the smaller Fold vehicles so they could spend weekends with their girlfriends.

Bram replied that they should contact Melisa and arrange for that to happen. They should also ask to stay in the facility where the Fold would deliver them.

He asked where the girl friends live and learned that one had a position as a Bank branch manager in Philadelphia and the other ran a small leather goods boutique in San Diego.

Bram asked if Zoe had vetted the two.

Negative Fold

Zoe replied that both Bob and Thomas had asked her to do that early in their romances.

Bram said that he gave them a green light and wished them well. He then pointed to the door and said that it was time to see what was for dinner.

END of the Preview

Continue reading in: Ripples In Time

Ron Mueller

About the Author

Ronald E. Mueller
remwriter95@gmail.com

Ron grew up in what is now Flint River State Park in Southeast Iowa. The 170-year-old house Ron lived in is built into a hillside. It faces a 125-foot-high cliff towering over the little Flint River. The house and the land talked to him about; the passing of time, the struggle to conquer the land, the struggles people faced and the wonder of nature.

He climbed the cliffs, crawled into the caves, dove from the swimming rock, collected clams from the bottom of the pond, gigged and skinned frogs for their legs. He trapped muskrats for fur, hunted raccoon in the dead of night, and with only a stick hunted rabbits in the dead of winter.

His young life was outdoors, and nature tested him.

He walked to a one room stone schoolhouse uphill both ways. A stern but warm-hearted teacher, Mrs. Henry was instrumental in shaping his character as she shepherded him from the fourth to the eighth grade. A Montessori before its time. It was a great way to grow up.

His experiences inter-twined with snippets of fantasy lend themselves to the adventures he leads the reader through.

Ron Mueller

Characters in: Negative Fold

Fold Characters

Amy	Wellington	NASA astronaut
Aanon	Zann	Swoosh Leader of the Alien's
Ada	Mouse	Einstein's children mice
Angela	Newton	Olivia Newton's Daughter
Bob		FBI bodyguards
Bonank	Etaing	Senator Senate Oversight Committee
Bram	Nielson	Protagonist
Castor	Suarez	Marine guard
Cedric	Stetson	Fishing boat
Celilo	Park	Fishing launch area, along Columbia River.
Charles	Ford	Science Advisor Senate Oversight Committee
Dalles		site in Oregon along Columbia River.
Danial	Bascom	Senator W Virginia Senate Oversight Committee
Daryl	Nazda	Backup Pilot Bubble 1 Pat Pilot
David	Conden	Utah Senator's partner
Dennison	Newton	Olivia Newton's Son
Donna		New Marine guard
Edward	Sharp	Site Marine Commander
Einstein	Mouse	Bram's first mouse
Einstein City		City on the Mataia
Elizabeth	Miller	humanist philosopher, .
Eric		FBI bodyguards
Erica	Wilson	Initial archrival
Ester	Mannerly	Nasa quality inspector for the two wheels.
Gerald	Gerry	Sooner Captain Erica's husband
Harold	Redat	Backup Pilot Bubble 2 Amy Pilot
Isaac	Mouse	Einstein's children mice
Jeffrey	Mikelson	Boss that is patient,
Jina	Juma	Mom
John	Morgan	NASA director Jefferies Boss
John	Stately	Senator Utah Senate Oversight Committee
Jose	Estrada	project manager wheel one and two

320

Negative Fold

Lacy	Stetson	first office support. Ted's daughter
Lester	Tilson	Marine Major General in charge of Fold security
Linda	Stetson	Ted's oldest becomes Bram's support.
Lori	Middleton	Lab, workshop supervisor
Luke	Stetson	Fishing boat Ted's son
Mallica	Evenston	World class mathematician
Marcus	Smith	World class astrophysicist
Marial	Stetson	Brought Picnic lunch -- Cedric's wife
Mary		Rushing River Inn Owner
Mataia	(Ma ta ee ah)	New world to which Bram moves
Melisa	Etrius	Organizer of the Fold neighborhood activities
Mike		Rushing River Inn Owner
Mt. Jefferson		hike & fishing, near to Rushing River
Myla	Smith	
Nuro	Juma	Dad
Ohaan	Toon	Bram's Alien equivalent
Olivia	Newton	Senator Maine Senate Oversight Committee
Orlando	Gutieres	Marine guard
Patricia	Fleming	NASA astronaut Bram's mate
Primeira	Planet	New Dry world to be used
Raymond		Daedlus Husband to be of Lacy
RCID	Geometric shp	rhombicosidodecahedron
Remi	Hardwood	Direct bubble assembly Lab technical
rhombicosidodecahedron		RCID shape of time & distance in neg Fold
Rita	Stetson	Brought Picnic lunch - Ted's wife
Samuel	Natorly	US President
Serena	Windal	Fold phycologist -Marine Therapist
Swoosh	Water Planet	Name of Alien Water world
Ted	Stetson	Fishing boat
Thomas		FBI bodyguards
USS Hood Wheel One		First Fold vessels
USS Rainier Wheel Two		First Fold vessels
Woo-an	Ang	Ohaan's mate
Zoe		FBI bodyguards
Zuri	Juma	Wheelchair bound autistic mental giant

Ron Mueller

Published by: Around the World Publishing LLC.

QR Links to
ATWP.US web site